Stones Under the Scythe

Cover and illustrations by
Olena Raspopova

Maps by
Stefan Slutsky

Stones Under the Scythe

Olha Mak

Translated by Vera Kaczmarskyj

iUniverse, Inc.
Bloomington

Stones Under the Scythe

iUniverse books may be ordered through booksellers or by contacting:

iUniverse
1663 Liberty Drive
Bloomington, IN 47403
www.iuniverse.com
1-800-Authors (1-800-288-4677)

ISBN: 978-1-4620-1037-0 (sc)
ISBN: 978-1-4620-1038-7 (hc)
ISBN: 978-1-4620-1039-4 (ebk)

Library of Congress Control Number: 2011905537

Printed in the United States of America

iUniverse rev. date: 11/09/2011

Dedicated to the millions of nameless martyrs—victims of the man-made famine (*Holodomor*) in Ukraine—on the fortieth anniversary 1933-1973) of this tragedy.[1]

---

[1] The author's dedication, as it appeared in the first Ukrainian-language edition of this book.

The Women's Association for the Defense of Four Freedoms for Ukraine, Inc. undertook this project in memory of the millions who perished in the man-made famine of 1932-1933, today known as *"Holodomor."* The recollections of several of our members, who had survived this genocide, made this a must project for our organization so that the youth of today would learn about a genocide that the world, for its convenience, tried to hide. Unfortunately, the world has not learned from the past and genocidal destruction of nations still continues even in the 21st century.

We would like to thank the daughter of Olha Mak, Ms. Myroslava Hec for granting us the right to undertake this project, Vera Kachmarskyj for her professional and artistic translation, where she brings forth the physical, psychological and emotional pain of the millions who perished or lived through this horror, Ihor Mirchuk for the introduction and editing, and Leo Iwaskiw for his editorial work.

We would like to acknowledge three of the trustees of the Ulana and Larysa Celewych Foundaton, Maria Lozynskyj, Luba Siletsky and Maria Wasylyk for initiating the project.

Larissa Lozynskyj-Kyj
Project Director
Women's Association for the Defense for Four Freedoms for Ukraine, Inc.

TO THE READER

From Myroslawa Hec (Olha Mak's daughter)

When reading this narrative, one has the impression that it tells the story of how disorganized the Soviet system was. In fact, nothing could be further from the truth. The famine was meticulously planned and flawlessly executed. People were given the false hope of survival and stood peacefully in queues day after day in the hope of staying alive. The truth was that there was not going to be enough food. The interminable waiting in queues in the winter cold would keep them busy, however, sapping their energy and leaving them with little will to organize or protest.

"Stones Under the Scythe," the title of this book in the original Ukrainian version, evokes a Ukrainian expression—"but the scythe hit a stone." It means that, in performing a task it was designed for, the tool (the scythe) hit upon unforeseen resistance that was difficult to cope with.

There were stones that Stalin's scythe could not crop.

CONTENTS

FOREWORD

Olha Mak, a prolific writer and author of several novels for adolescents and young adults, wrote *Stones Under the Scythe*[2] to help shatter a conspiracy of silence and deliberate denial about one of the most terrible tragedies to befall any nation, a catastrophe caused by the workings of a group of fanatical "creators of a new breed of men." We do not know whether the characters of Mak's novel actually existed, but her narrative is based on real events that she herself had witnessed as a 20-year old student living during the time of these events in the city of Kharkiv. The story of 15 year-old Andriy (Andrew) recreates the fate of millions of Ukrainian children who either perished or barely escaped death in the years of a man-made famine, *Holodomor*, that took the life of every fourth Ukrainian—7 to 10 million altogether, 3 million of them children.

Ukraine, at the time of this story, was teeming with children engaged in a desperate struggle to escape the clutches of death that enveloped the entire Ukrainian countryside after it was depleted of every morsel of food. Like Andriy, many of those children managed to slip into Ukraine's cities, where famine was not so severe, but which were off limits to them. Like Andriy, many of them were the sons and daughters of industrious and experienced farmers who had been thrown out of their homes by communist activists several years earlier, and left to die as dispossessed outcasts (officially, they

---

[2]   Originally published in Ukrainian under the title, *Kaminnia pid kosoyu* (Stones Under the Scythe).

xiii

would be labeled as "kurkuls"[3]). Threats of arrest kept neighbors from extending a helping hand to them although, in a matter of just 2-3 years most Ukrainian farmers, left unharmed by that first onslaught, would themselves be stripped of the most basic requirement for survival—food.

For Ukrainians, "1933" is not just a year, or an abbreviated designation of a singular calamity (such as "9/11"). It is, rather, an expression that stirs up haunting reminders of the power and sinister willingness of an inhuman government to destroy millions of people under the guise of creating a "new communist society." Ukrainians remember 1933 as the year when their entire nation found itself on the verge of extinction as the result of a plot that had the marks of genocide. The villages that children like Andriy left behind became virtual ghost towns, populated by skeletal shadows of inhabitants, who only a few months earlier were well-fed, vivacious, and full of creative energy. Survivors relate how an eerie silence fell over Ukrainian villages during the height of the Famine. There were no sounds of children shouting as they do when they play with one another, no loquacious chatter among neighbors, not even any barking of dogs, meowing of cats, or even chirping of birds since most of the dogs, cats, and birds were captured and devoured by starving farmers.

Ukraine, it is well to recall, is the East European country that once was known as the "breadbasket of Europe." It is a very fertile land with half of its territory covered by black soil ("*chornozem*"), which, under proper care, can produce high yields of every type of crop. Seven thousand years ago, one of the first agricultural societies in the world appeared on this territory. The fertile soil ensured bountiful harvests for thousands of years. Ukraine possessed the wherewithal to avoid widespread famines. Even during times of severe drought that occurred once in several decades, only certain regions would be seriously affected and hungry farmers from those

---

[3]   Better known by its Russian-language equivalent—"kulaks."

areas would be able to travel elsewhere to obtain food for survival.

But the *Holodomor* of 1932-1933 was not the result of natural causes. Official reports from those years indicate that there was no drought then and the harvest was quite bountiful. Newly discovered documents, kept secret until recently, offer increasing evidence of what Ukrainians have known for a long time: this famine was man-made. It was engineered at the connivance of Soviet dictator Joseph Stalin and his henchmen.[4] Numerous deaths, resulting from hunger, began to be noted by village officials soon after Ukrainian farmers were forced to deliver exorbitant quantities of grain to the communist state. Then, in the autumn of 1932, virtually every household in the countryside was ransacked by communist activists, who rummaged through storage bins, cracked open the walls of houses, and burrowed through yards with picks in search of "hidden food."

---

[4]   In 2008, the Security Service of Ukraine (SBU), disclosed 3,685 heretofore classified Soviet government and secret service (NKVD) documents, including several bearing Joseph Stalin's signature, which serve as evidence that the 1932-1933 *Holodomor* was directed at the Ukrainian people and other groups deemed dangerous by Stalin and his henchmen. Alongside of this, excavations were conducted at 933 mass burial sites that lay concealed for many decades. The documents reveal the mechanisms employed for carrying out this genocide: the full seizure of crops in fields and of food stored in people's houses by party activists sent from Russia, the virtual blockade of Ukrainian territory by special armed units, the placement of numerous districts on black lists of areas which were subjected to a trade blockade and sealed off from being able to receive any kind of food provisions, restrictions on the movement of farmers looking for food and a ban on travel for peasants who tried to cross from Ukraine into Russia in search of food and survival. In 2009, a court in Kyiv posthumously tried and convicted those Communist Party functionaries against whom there is clear evidence that they spearheaded the actions that led to the *Holodomor* (genocidal famine) against the Ukrainian people and thus committed crimes against humanity.

The first victims of the famine were the very young and the elderly, the age groups whose organisms are the most vulnerable when undernourished. Reports from administrators, transmitted at the beginning of the new school year in September 1933, revealed that two thirds of Ukraine's pupils were missing from school rolls. Eventually, the scythe of death spared no age group and no aid was forthcoming. So, as their parents helplessly attempted to preserve the life of their youngest children, thousands of adolescents and young adults ventured to make their way from the countryside into Ukraine's cities where at least there were stores that occasionally sold bread and other foodstuffs. Foreign diplomats stationed in Kharkiv, then the capital of Soviet Ukraine, reported to their respective governments that hundreds of corpses were picked up from the streets each day. One secret government report, written in the spring of 1933, revealed that there were 18,000 homeless children living on the streets of Kharkiv. Scores of those children perished each and every day, only to be replaced by others. Another report recorded more than 300,000 homeless children in the Kyiv region. Orphanages and children's shelters were too overcrowded to take them in. We can only surmise their fate.

The cities were much less affected by the *Holodomor* because they were populated mainly by non-Ukrainians due to a history of discrimination against Ukrainians attempting to set up businesses in cities as well as to the traditional Ukrainian attachment to an agricultural way of life. It was not easy to enter cities at the time of the *Holodomor* because police units were ordered to block villagers from making their way there, just as army units were deployed along Ukraine's border to prevent farmers from migrating into Russia where, though there were food shortages, there was not the wide-scale famine that was ravaging Ukraine.

What led to this sinister plot against the Ukrainian people? The answer lies in the nature of the Ukrainian people, which we find personified by the main characters of Olha Mak's novel. People like young Andriy Pivpola and the middle-aged widow, Lidia Serhiyivna, were considered dangerous and inherently alien to the society that Communist despots like Stalin and Lenin before him were aiming to create. Hardy individuals, such as Andriy and Lidia, embodied the essence of the Ukrainian people—fiercely independent, individualistic, hard working, deeply moral and spiritual in disposition. Andriy represents a long line of Ukrainian farmers who passed their noble spirit onto their descendants by a culturally rich way of life, which they had fought to preserve despite efforts by numerous foreign occupiers to destroy it. Certainly, the Russian Communist regime needed hard-working people to labor in the fields from which it bled the crops that provided its empire with the money to purchase industrial equipment from the West. But the Communists wanted servile workers and not people who live as true Ukrainians have lived for ages—with God, country, and love of the land as an integral part of their spirit.

Lidia Serhiyivna, Andriy's savior, personifies the depleted ranks of well-educated Ukrainians who were active in cultural and intellectual professions. The totalitarian Soviet machine had wiped out most members of the Ukrainian elite or banished them to distant concentration camps yet in 1930. Consequently, by the watershed years of 1932-1933 the Soviets had wiped out all segments of society, viewed as having the potential for mobilizing Ukraine's large population for resistance to their schemes. The next act of this drama was focused on the farmers who Stalin believed were the foundation and heart of Ukrainian society. His aim was to assure that a Ukrainian nation with its own identity, culture, and aspirations would cease to exist.

The story of Ukraine's *Holodomor*, was a forbidden topic for virtually all the years in which the Soviet empire existed. People were still being arrested in the 1980s and given prison sentences of several years simply for talking about it. Needless to say, the *Holodomor* of 1933 had tragic consequences for the Ukrainian people. No event in history has had as devastating an effect on Ukrainians as this man-made catastrophe. Survivors, historians, sociologists, and older observers of Ukrainian life all lament that so much of the Ukrainian spirit, cultural heritage, songs, and customs vanished with the *Holodomor* of 1933. The most productive and creative segments of society were wiped out and have not been replaced to this day. In southern and eastern Ukraine, the Ukrainian population was decimated and today those parts are populated mainly by non-Ukrainians. For all of these reasons, scholars characterize this calamity as genocide. [5]

However, in spite of everything, Olha Mak's novel is not a somber story of horrible events. The characters of her story bear witness to the truth that the human spirit cannot be fully subdued. But this is a truth that needs frequent reminders, for everyone at some point comes to feel crushed by the brutality that confronts them.

Mak's story actually ends sixty years after the *Holodomor* of 1933. Having endured centuries of incessant blows to its existence, the Ukrainian people were somehow able to muster enough strength to take advantage of the rapidly developing events that marked the fall of Soviet power to proclaim

---

[5]   It is also worth noting here that Raphael Lemkin, who coined the term "genocide" and helped bring about passage of international laws defining and criminalizing genocide, himself wrote an essay entitled "Soviet Genocide in Ukraine." In it he delineated four stages of the Ukrainian genocide, each directed at one of the groups or institutions that constituted the core of the Ukrainian nation. "The third prong of the Soviet plan was aimed at the farmers, the large mass of independent peasants who are the repository of the tradition, folklore and music, the national language and literature, the national spirit, of Ukraine... The weapon used against this body is perhaps the most terrible of all—starvation. This is not simply a case of mass murder. It is a case of genocide, of destruction, not of individuals only, but of a culture and a nation."

their independence in 1991. It was the revelations about the *Holodomor* of 1933 and the stirring of a haunting, though subdued, memory that convinced many wavering individuals that this was the only path that Ukrainians could choose for themselves and their descendants.

Ihor Mirchuk, Ph.D.
Philadelphia, PA
July 2010

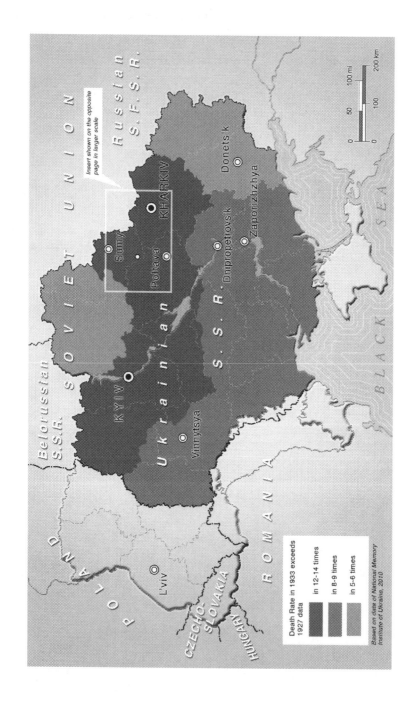

Insert shown on the opposite
page in larger scale

Russian
S.F.S.R.

S O V I E T   U N I O N

Russian S.F.S.R.

Donets'k

Zaporizhzhya

KHARKIV

Sumy

Dnipropetrovs'k

Poltava

U k r a i n i a n   S. S. R.

Belorussian
S.S.R.

KYIV

Vinnytsya

B L A C K

S E A

P O L A N D

L'viv

CZECHO-
SLOVAKIA

HUNGARY

R O M A N I A

Death Rate in 1933 exceeds
1927 data

in 12-14 times

in 8-9 times

in 5-6 times

*Based on data of National Memory
Institute of Ukraine, 2010*

200 km

100 mi

100

50

100

0

0

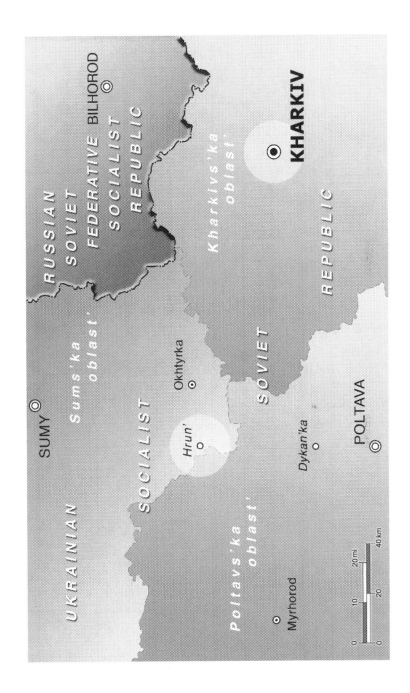

1

The smell of rotting corpses hung in the air as the legal residents of Kharkiv, the capital of Ukraine, carried on their plucky and brutal struggle for existence. Some of these city dwellers spent their days at work, others in queues—at stores, at fuel supply depots, at tram stops, and in front of various government offices. These latter were always in a hurry, always angry, always quarrelsome, and cursed the government at every step. They hated every person ahead of them in line with a passion that, in more normal times, would have been reserved exclusively for one's worst enemies.

Besides these "legal residents," there was in the city that year another group of people, possibly even more numerous than the first. This was the group of people with no *propyska* (the registration necessary for the right to live in the city) and thus with no rights. Members of this group no longer seemed to fit into any definition of "citizen." Unlike the city's legal residents, people with no *propyska* had no reason to hurry or quarrel. They did not mill around at the stores—they had no ration cards. They did not stand in line for heating fuel—they had no homes to heat. They had no reason to push their way into overcrowded trams to secure a place—they had no place to go. And their relationship to the government was so bad that it was best they stayed as far away as possible from all government offices. To make a long story short, they were Ukraine's *kurkuls* (*kulaks* in Russian)—the "saboteurs of collectivization," the "enemies of Soviet power." Popularly, they were known simply as "the starving." Although "the starving", by virtue of their numbers, were the defining feature of Kharkiv's landscape that year, providing the city with its distinctive character and smell (thanks to them the air reeked of decaying flesh), they were the most voiceless and unheard element in the city. "The starving" were quiet. They were reticent. They were subdued. Quietly they wandered the streets; quietly they sat propped up in front of buildings and against fences. Timidly they stretched out their hands for alms. Silently they died

1

by the thousands, fading from this earth as shadows fade into the dark, as markings of sand fade in the wind, as a despairing cry fades over a rocky mountain top. They were dying out . . . .

That they were dying was not strange. What was strange was that they were still alive at all. How did they live—where and on what? Where did they manage to hide their emaciated, famine-ridden bodies from the merciless cold? They had no houses. They did not even have the burrows that animals in the wild have to protect them from the wintry cold. One would have thought a single cold night of the northern wind's snake-like hissing would have put an end to the suffering that starvation dragged out for weeks. But no! The night passed and the morning's generous harvest of corpses made hardly any difference at all, for masses of new martyrs appeared—seemingly out of nowhere—to take the place of those carted away in the only queue still open to them—the queue to death. Now it was the newcomers' turn to wind their way in unsteady drunken-like steps along the streets, to stretch out their hands for alms as they sat on the frozen ground, backs propped up against the cold of fences and buildings. The look on their faces bore witness to the fact that they had crossed over the line in which pain still had any power at all. All around, people were passing them by—some hurrying to work, others to secure a place in some queue, many engaged in a spirited discussion about the likelihood of receiving a larger—or smaller!—ration of bread that day, or about the quality of the herring they had managed to procure with great difficulty just the day before, or about the price of the rubber boots purchased on the black market.

In addition to these two key categories of people in the city, there was another group residing in the city—the criminals. These were the government officials, those who enforced the State's criminal policies, and who ordered the killings and the pillaging "in line with the law." They did so with the flourish of a modern-day Genghis Khan. This work brought them respect and glory, and won them praise. These people were referred to as "comrade so-and-so" of "such-and-such a rank." They were the recipients of government awards and Orders of Distinction. They were widely celebrated. Newspapers wrote about them regularly, and printed their photographs. They were well dressed, these official criminals, in the warm overcoats and fur hats and carried the obligatory large leather briefcases that were the uniform of their class . . . .

There was another group of criminals—the *blats*, or common criminals. They were barely distinguishable from the masses of the starving. Like them, they were dressed in rags. Like them, they were unkempt. Like them, they were homeless. Unlike the official criminals—the "comrades" in government office—these petty criminals were not a respected group in society. No one heaped praise on them. No one spoke of them with respect. They were referred to as *blats*. They had no power; they did all their dirty work themselves. In truth, however, this group rarely pillaged in the full sense of the word. They killed rarely, and then only in the most extreme circumstances and primarily for revenge. As for petty stealing . . . Well! They stole at every step. Of course, by comparison with the "comrades" with large leather briefcases and well-fed visages, these were ne'er-do-well petty criminals who traded in ludicrously small things—a piece of bread, a bit of clothing, a wallet stuffed with worthless paper money. Of course, when their efforts were not successful, they were often repaid with bruises, bloodied faces or broken ribs by their intended victims. These incidents, however, were rarely reported in the press.

These were the four categories of people—inhabitants of the then-capital of the Ukrainian Soviet Socialist Republic, who were going about their very separate lives in Kharkiv, situated on the steppes of Ukraine, during this most inhospitable time.

Andriy did not belong to any of these groups. He had run away from a half-demolished, poorly heated, lice-infested, smelly, hungry, and overcrowded orphanage just a week earlier. He was new to the city. He fled the orphanage because he could not tolerate life there any longer. Though wise and mature beyond his years, he came to this decision only on the vaguest of hopes of finding a better life elsewhere. He held on to this hope during the four days it took to walk to the city. His hope did not waver when he joined the ranks of first one, and then another, and yet another group of beggared peasants, who looked ever so much like corpses summoned from their graves by the Last Judgment call, as they inched their way toward the city.

Indeed, Andriy had uncommon luck. In the four days of his journey, he managed to have not one, but two, good meals. Each time he ate until he was fully satiated. His first meal was with a group that was just finishing off a slaughtered old nag. The second—when he found a potato bush snuggled under a cover of snow which, by some miracle, had gone unnoticed. Eleven huge potatoes! True, the horsemeat had been tough and sinewy and the potatoes frozen. But grilled over a fire, the potatoes were a feast for his not-very-exacting stomach, and left him feeling revived and hopeful.

Andriy fully understood why people were fleeing the villages for the city. There were no forcible grain collections in the city, no collectivization, no special taxes, like the penalty yield tax.[6] People were not being forcibly de-*kurkulized* (de-*kulakized*) in the city, nor were they being thrown out of their houses or forced to choose between joining a collective farm and exile to Siberia. Moreover, the city offered the prospect of work in a variety of factories and shops. What was more, people said that the city had bread for sale for everyone. Surely, he would find a way to manage!

The sight of Kharkiv, however, when Andriy finally managed to reach the city just before nightfall, shattered all his hopes. A great weight descended on him. Could there really be so many starving people? Their numbers were overwhelming! They were like swarms of aphids on a cabbage leaf! How could there be enough factories and work places even in the city to employ them? What bakery could bake enough bread to feed them all?

Discouraged, he wound his way aimlessly down the streets, feeling his spirits sink further at every corner. Had he lost his way in a dark and dense forest his despair would not have been as deep. Everything around him was foreign, inexplicable, and therefore frightening. He did not know where to begin, and he understood that it would be ludicrous to turn to anyone for any advice.

In terror he passed frightening-looking individuals and groups—all doomed to a slow death. Only now did he become aware of the full scope and scale of the tragedy he had seen only snippets and fragments of before. Had he really hoped to find salvation here? Stupid, stupid!

The sun was setting. Andriy kept on walking. He walked past buildings and across streets, cursing himself all the while for God knows what. He was no longer thinking about work, or even food. His only thought was how to survive that night. Where to rest his head? Where to hide from the cold? How to stay alive until morning?

---

[6]   An exploitative tax the new government imposed on peasants who fell behind in paying their regular taxes. It was 5 and even 10 times greater than the regular tax rate.

Andriy was walking by a large, multi-storied building, with a big pile of coal in front of it, when he caught fragments of a conversation.

"What to do? You can go on working till midnight, or stay up, keeping watch over the coal. Otherwise, all sorts of vermin will carry it away bit by bit and there won't be a trace of it left by morning, and I will be dragged to court and put on trial."[7]

"You should not have accepted the delivery. You should not have signed for it!"

"Not signed for it? Then the school would have been left without any fuel. As it is, this delivery was long overdue. If I had refused it, they wouldn't have come back another time. They'd say, 'we came and you refused to take it!'"

"But that's not your problem, it's management's problem."

Two men were talking among themselves. One of them held a metal box in his hand and looked like a laborer on his way home from work. The other, wearing an old coat closed at the waist by an old belt, was shoveling coal into two dented and shapeless buckets.

Andriy had walked quite far past them when he had an idea. He retraced his steps. The men were no longer standing at the gate. Andriy saw the back of one of them halfway down the street. He guessed that the other must have taken the pails of coal inside, leaving the gate ajar behind him. Indeed, that man soon came back and shot Andriy an unfriendly glance as he began to shovel coal into the pails again.

"*Diad'ku,*[8] said Andriy shyly. "Would you like me to help you?"

The man gave him an even more hostile look.

"Scat! Get away from here!" he answered angrily. "Humph! A helper! And where will I get the money to pay you?"

"I am not asking for money," the boy hurriedly explained. "My only request is for a place to sleep tonight."

"Get out of here before I take a swing at you!" said the man, losing his patience. "A 'place to sleep!' Oh yes, we know you *blats* very well."

---

[7] It was not uncommon during these times for people to be put on trial for stealing "government property." Typically, they had no way to defend themselves.

[8] Literally, "uncle"—a respectful term commonly used when addressing a person who is significantly one's senior.

Andriy bristled at these words and took a step forward towards the man, and shot back in anger:

"Don't you dare call me a *blat* or I will forget that you are an elderly man and smash my fist into your face so hard that you will lose your balance! I'll have you know I am the son of honest folk! I've never so much as touched a piece of straw that wasn't mine! Nor have I ever put my hand out looking for charity! If I were a *blat*, I would have found myself a place to sleep for nothing. Good day to you!" He turned on his heel and left.

"Hey you!" shouted the man after him. "Come back!"

Andriy retraced his steps.

"Well," said the man in a kinder tone, "if you want to help—please do. I'll let you sleep in the basement. There are lots of empty bags there. You won't freeze."

Silently, Andriy took the shovel from the old man, and began shoveling. Once the pails were full, he asked, "Where do I take this coal?"

"Follow me."

The entrance to the basement was behind the building. As they walked, the man began to tell Andriy a little about himself. His name was Mykola Savchenko and he was a live-in guard and caretaker at the school. He had a wife, and she worked alongside him at the school. Both of them were semi-invalids, a word Savchenko pronounced with a bit of a lisp. There was a story behind how they came to be here.

It was all because of an unfortunate accident. Savchenko and his wife were traveling by cart one day when their horses were startled by a passing truck and bolted. The cart was totally wrecked, and the Savchenkos themselves were so badly hurt that they each spent half a year in the hospital. At first the government awarded them a disability pension, but then a panel of doctors deemed them capable of doing light work. So they assigned them to the school where . . . Listening with only half an ear, Andriy interrupted Savchenko in mid-sentence.

"We need two more buckets or some kind of bag. Then we'll be able to divvy up our work. One of us will fill the pails. The other will carry them to the basement. We are just wasting time walking back and forth together like this."

They couldn't find another pail, but did manage to get a sturdy bag.

"I see you are not stupid," said the man appreciatively. "This is just a fraction of the coal needed to heat a building of this size. But hauling and storing even this amount in the basement is not a small task. A person working alone could easily work well past midnight without getting the job done!"

They worked on. At first they took turns—one filled the pails, the other carried them to the basement. Andriy soon noticed, however, that the old man almost buckled under the weight of the pails. So he instructed him to keep filling the buckets and the bag as full as possible while he carried—practically ran!—them to the basement himself.

Even though both worked steadily and hard, Savchenko found a way to keep up his litany of complaints.

"They call this 'light work!' But it is not so light to sweep twelve classrooms a day. Just moving the desks from one side of the room to the other is back-breaking. Then there are the corridors, two conference rooms, the faculty room, and the steps! Once a year all the floors in the building have to be polished with black mineral oil. In the autumn, the windows need to be washed and caulked. In spring, they need to be unsealed and washed again.

"Last spring, my wife fell off the ladder and hurt her foot so badly that she is still limping even now. And winter! What to say? In addition to all our other work, there's wood to be chopped for the fire. And coal to be carried to and from the basement and loaded into each fireplace.

"The students leave every day at two. That's when our work begins. My wife and I work till midnight, and still the job is not done. Often as not we have to get up at dawn to finish up. True, for this we get a roof over our head and don't have to pay for fuel and electricity. All the same, it's hard work. And yet, when it comes to the food allotted to us—our ration cards are stamped 'light work' employees, so we get less rations than regular workers."

He continued in this vein—spitting, cursing and carrying on angrily, as if hoping that in so doing he would be able to dislodge a heavy weight from his soul.

Finally the job was done. Andriy carefully put the pails back in their places, shook out the bag, and swept away all traces of black coal off the pavement.

"Is that it or is there anything else?" he asked.

"Thank you, lad. That's all," Savchenko replied, tapping his foot in indecision.

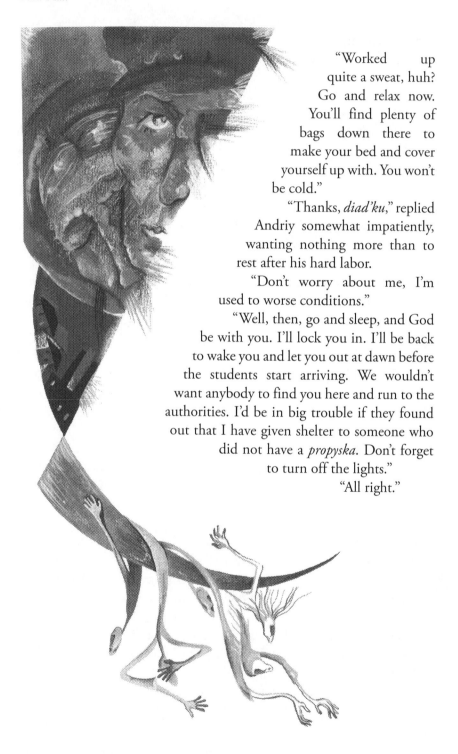

"Worked up quite a sweat, huh? Go and relax now. You'll find plenty of bags down there to make your bed and cover yourself up with. You won't be cold."

"Thanks, *diad'ku*," replied Andriy somewhat impatiently, wanting nothing more than to rest after his hard labor.

"Don't worry about me, I'm used to worse conditions."

"Well, then, go and sleep, and God be with you. I'll lock you in. I'll be back to wake you and let you out at dawn before the students start arriving. We wouldn't want anybody to find you here and run to the authorities. I'd be in big trouble if they found out that I have given shelter to someone who did not have a *propyska*. Don't forget to turn off the lights."

"All right."

Savchenko left, turning the key twice in the lock, and padded away to another part of the building. Andriy turned off the lights and with great satisfaction dove into the warmth of the bags. Every bone in his body ached from the hard work, for his body was weak from malnourishment. His insides were screaming with hunger. Still, he thanked God that he was not out wandering the streets aimlessly, that he was not out in the night, dying in the cold.

Before Andriy had much of a chance for further reflection, he heard the man's limping gait along the corridor again. Again the key turned twice in the lock.

"He's come to throw me out!" Andriy thought, frightened, bracing himself for a confrontation. But the man had come for a totally different reason.

"Hey there, lad!" he called from the threshold in the dark. "Come to the house!"

"Why?" asked Andriy in a none-too-happy voice. "I'm fine here."

"Don't be afraid, and stop talking nonsense. How can you be fine on a totally empty stomach? My wife has sent me to invite you to dinner."

Andriy was up and ready to go in the blink of an eye.

"Thank you! Thank you!" he cried out with emotion. "My insides are making such a racket that they could rival the blaring marching music played at the October Revolution commemoration parade!"

Savchenko's "house," if that's the word for it, was a very ordinary space under the stairs of the school. It measured 2 by 3 meters at the level part before the wall slanted sharply down under the stairs. The furniture was one tiny table, a lopsided iron bed, and a homemade stove-like contraption which doubled as a heater. The stove was red-hot and the room was so warm that the door had to be kept ajar.

Entering, Andriy took off his hat, made the sign of the cross (even though there was no icon on any of the bare walls) and greeted the lady of the house.

"Sit down, son," said the woman kindly. "You will be our guest tonight. '*Chym khata bahata, tym rada*' (*With whatever our house is rich—we are ready to share with our guest*).[9] It's just that our house is so 'rich' at the

---

[9]   *Chym khata bahata, tym rada.* This is a very common expression among Ukrainians when guests drop in unexpectedly.

9

moment," she went on, "that we can't even offer you a crumb of bread. There's been no bread in the stores for a whole week now. We are fed on promises. 'Tomorrow,' they say, 'we're sure to have bread tomorrow.' I wonder: when they finally deliver the bread, will they give us extra loaves for the days that were missed? We work so hard for those crumbs and stand waiting for them in those endless lines for two-three hours at a time. Often, very often, we come away empty-handed."

"Natalka, please. Stop talking so much!" said her husband, cutting her off. "Please give us whatever you have there to eat. I'm so hungry that my very soul is howling!"

The woman set a metal teapot on the table and dropped a piece of chicory into the boiling water. She took down three sturdy glasses from the shelf and a rather large bowl full of some sort of blackish dumplings. Then she unwrapped a small lump of sugar and carefully divided it into three equal parts, placing a sliver beside each glass.

All the while, Andriy was taking a closer look at his new acquaintances. Both were over forty, both were very thin, both limped, though the limp of the lady of the house was more pronounced than her husband's. She had a bruise on her forehead as well.

"Here lad, help yourself," said Savchenko, pouring chicory-colored hot water into his glass. "More often than not, our meals now consist of these imitation pork chops. We no longer take our tea like the Russians, who put a lump of sugar or a teaspoon of marmalade on their tongues to sweeten the hot liquid as they sip. No, our new way of drinking tea is consistent with the times: we gaze at the sugar while sipping our tea, letting the sight of it sweeten our imaginations and our tea. By the way, have you ever eaten pork chops like these before?"

"No," admitted Andriy, happily biting down on one of them. "But I think I remember my mother talking about them once."

"Really? Your mother mentioned them? Did your family raise pigs?"

"Of course we did. We always slaughtered a piglet for Christmas."

"And what did you feed your pigs?" the man pressed on, pretending not to know.

"Leave the boy alone, Mykola. Let him eat!"

"Just a minute, Natalka!" persisted the man. "People need to be enlightened. Now then, what did your family feed the pigs?"

Andriy continued to chew on his food and sip his boiling hot water, leaving the sugar for dessert.

"Well, you know," he said, barely able to talk with his mouth so full, "first we would feed them pumpkins. Then, as the seasons changed, we would give them small potatoes or beets. In our house we used to cook up a huge kettle of feed into which we stirred mashed potatoes and chaff, adding some whey to increase the pigs' appetite so they would eat more and gain more weight."

"Yes, yes!" chuckled Savchenko with glee. "That's exactly right. They used to add whey to the feed so the pigs would eat better and gain more weight. Then, once they slaughtered the pig, they would make sausages, cure the bacon, and bake the hams. And for those who'd want to sample some of the fresh meat, they'd cut off a slice, pound it well with a little mallet, season it with a little pepper, add some onions and fry it in some lard. Only now we eat the food farmers used to feed to their pigs. Except for the potatoes. We simply cannot afford them. We eat only the potato peels. Just a week ago, my wife bought half a bag of them and a bag of chaff. She boiled the potato peel, ground it up, stirred in the chaff, made the patties and fried them up on a skillet and the result—'pork-style' chops!' Hmm, we nourish ourselves better on them than your pigs once did, you see?"

His joke was more sad than funny, and the lady of the house let out a sigh. Her husband, meanwhile, raised his voice in a parody of a Soviet propaganda ditty.

"Oh, this is truly heaven, and not mere life!
Nothing to do, but lay down and die!"

He muttered a curse word, swung his hand in a gesture of frustration, and attacked his food.

His wife ate sparingly, all the while encouraging Andriy to eat more. As he ate, she asked him about his life—about his family, his place of birth. Andriy was not in a very talkative mood, however. He mentioned only that he was an orphan and that he had fled from an orphanage in order to come to Kharkiv to find a job. Savchenko shook his head disapprovingly.

"That was not a wise move on your part, Andriy. You should have stayed at the orphanage."

"No! To hell with that orphanage!" said Andriy, scowling. "You think we were fed there? Earlier, they would feed us watery broth and a slice of bread twice a day. But then it became so overcrowded that they had to throw out the beds and make everyone sleep, helter-skelter, on the floors. More often than not the kitchen stayed closed for two days in a row. When it opened, there was only food enough for about half the children. And even they got only half a ladle of broth each. The rest went hungry. What's more, there was no bread to be had at all. What bread was delivered was divvied up among the personnel. If a little was left over for the orphans, they had to fight for it amongst themselves. Only the most brutal ones ended up getting any. There were many children at the orphanage with bellies swollen from malnutrition. No, there was no reason to stay."

"Still," Savchenko pressed on, "you might have gotten a morsel of bread from time to time there. You are a strong boy. I'm sure you know how to fend for yourself. I'll tell you honestly, it will be much worse here. Go back!"

"No, I will not," replied Andriy, lifting his head like a spirited horse. "Even if I went back, they would not take me. In the past, they had to use force to keep the orphans from running away. Back then the orphanage was almost like a prison. But now they turn away even the children that are brought in by the police. If an orphan runs away these days, it is cause for celebration, for there is one less mouth to feed!"

Savchenko sighed deeply and busied himself with rolling a cigarette.

"It seems that no matter what one does—a step forward, a step back—the result is always the same—death," he said darkly, sucking in the foul-smelling smoke.

"Stop cawing, Mykola!" remonstrated his wife. "You see that the boy is bright and not afraid of work. It's not possible that he won't find a job in all of Kharkiv."

Her husband turned to her and said with real anger, "What times are you living in? Don't you know how things are today? There are millions just like him looking for work. You know how it is with officials today! They won't give you a job unless you have a *propyska* (the registration necessary for the right to live in the city). And you can't get a *propyska* without a job. Moreover, you have to sign a 'statement about your social background,' known as a *dovidka*. Anyone with eyes can see that his 'social background' is one that will get him nowhere. It's the same with all those poor souls wandering, and dying, on our city's streets today."

"One can't get a word in edgewise with you," said the woman, now angry herself. "Yes, I know many are dying. But many also manage to hang on to something and survive! Look at Mykhailenko's brother. He and his entire family managed to get a *propyska*."

"Mykhailenko succeeded only because he had a brother living here already. And what a brother! That man really knows how to get around. He can run rings around not one but two devils and get his own way!" replied her husband angrily, but with a hint of admiration in his voice.

"Perhaps we should seek his advice?" asked his wife timidly.

"That would be a waste of time. Myklhailenko's brother was not stupid either. He did not come empty-handed from the village, as Andriy has from the orphanage. They were able to give generous bribes. As a result, they could get what they needed to establish themselves here. But this boy has neither a brother, nor any documents, nor a *khabar* (a bribe). What can we do?!" Savchenko let out a dejected sigh.

Andriy hung his head sadly. He felt despondent. Truly, there was nobody he could lean on in this big terrifying city. Here were two well-meaning people, but they could not give him much hope. There were millions out there just like him! Dear God, was he really like one of those doomed people he passed so timorously on the streets? He did not want to even think of himself as one of them, he did not want to stretch out his hand for alms, or to die, propped up against some fence like them. He wanted to live, to work, to buy bread, to have enough money to buy at least the ingredients for the "pork chops" he was served for dinner this evening. This was why he had fled the orphanage. Had he reached his goal only to discover that he was one of millions, who thought and felt just as he did, that they had covered all those snow-filled and windswept miles only to meet their death? So he wasn't an exception?

As if reading his thoughts, Savchenko suddenly clapped him on the back.

"But don't you worry, Andriy!" he said with forced gaiety. "Don't resort to evil. Go out, talk with people, and keep trying. It will not be easy, but my wife is right—some do manage to find a way. I would gladly have you stay with us, but it is against the rules, and ours is a government apartment. As you see, we ourselves have little to eat. However, though we might not have even buns as meager as these to offer you to eat, I will always let you in to spend the night. Only mind you come after twilight and make sure no one is around as you enter. One more word of warning: have nothing to do with the *blats*. Though they might offer a way of survival, you will surely lose your soul with them. You would not want to spend the rest of your days in some prison in Siberia. It would be better to die straightaway."

13

Andriy had to restrain himself to respond politely. He did not want to speak in anger to this hospitable man.

"If that's what I'd wanted, I could have joined the *blats* in the orphanage and divvied up bread rations with them back then. But it seems that I was not born to be a criminal."

"I know, Andriy. But life now is so difficult, that . . . ," began Savchenko, letting his voice trail away. He got up and led Andriy to the basement to sleep.

2

Snuggled in the warmth of the bags, Andriy fell into a deep sleep and dreamed wispy cobweb-like dreams through the night. Savchenko was able to wake him at dawn only with great difficulty.

"Wake up, son! Wake up!" he called, shaking Andriy. "You've overslept! People are on their way to work already. Go out among them and ask around. Working people will know where additional help might be needed. Someone might even offer to take you along. Here," he said, dropping some coins into Andriy's hand, "tram fare."

Still half-asleep, Andriy stood shaking with cold, his teeth chattering. It took him a while to remember where he was and to absorb what the man was saying to him.

"Hurry! Hurry! And remember: if you don't find anything, come back here again tonight to sleep."

It was still dark outside. Stars twinkled high above. The city was waking up. One could hear the sound of tram bells in the distance, the sound of muffled footsteps on the frozen ground, the sound of people's voices. Opening the gate, Savchenko suddenly took a quick step back.

"Oh! Another frozen one!" he said without a hint of emotion. He could have been talking about a lump of coal. "This is the fifth person so far who has given up his spirit here," he continued. "They seem to like to prop themselves up at this gate. And now I, Savchenko, will have to run to the police station and file a report. They'll want to send someone to cart the body away before the students start arriving. As if the students are unaware of what's happening all around them."

Still muttering, he bent over the dead body and moved it away from the entrance with great difficulty.

"Dear God!" he said and sighed when he was done.

Andriy had seen hundreds of dead bodies in his life—some back in his village, some at the orphanage, many more on his way to Kharkiv. He'd seen so many that the shock and the novelty had worn off long ago. But this time was different. He got so rattled by the dead body at the gate that he forgot not only to thank the caretaker but even to say goodbye. Instead, he quickly jumped out into the street and walked—almost ran—for a long time in whatever direction his feet carried him.

The cold cut through his body. His jaws were aching. The steam of every breath he let out turned to frost and settled on his chest. On and on he ran, not knowing whether he was running to try to keep warm or to put as much distance as possible between himself and the frozen body at the gate. Out of the corners of his eyes he saw other contorted figures, whitened with frost. One . . . . Another . . . . And yet another . . . . A group huddled together, motionless, covered in a thin sheet of frost. Frozen! All of them had met their end at this very place where he was hoping to find a new beginning. Andriy tried to avoid looking at them. Every new creak of an opening gate and every shadowy figure walking through it filled him with unspeakable dread. They all seemed like the walking dead.

Everything about his surroundings appeared gloomier this morning, and more foreign and terrifying than the night before. As he ran, the tall street lights alongside the road and the yellowish light they cast began to look like candles all lit up and standing guard on either side of an interminably long coffin that was the street. How to find a way out? Was there a way out? No, he thought in despair. He felt death surrounding him, gazing down on him through hollow eyes from every direction, taunting him with a mirthless, inaudible laugh. He ran faster, coming to a dead stop and out of his maudlin reverie only when he nearly collided with a group of people. Looking around, he saw that they were waiting at a tram stop, all clad in cloth boots, and all probably on their way to work. Andriy took his place at the end of the line.

After a while, he pulled on the sleeve of the man in front of him, and asked,

"*Diad'ku*, are you on your way to work?"

The man turned around and looked at Andriy in surprise.

"And what do you think? That I'm off on a hike?" he replied jeeringly.

"May I come with you?" Andriy pressed on, ignoring the unpleasant tone. "I'm looking for a job."

The man pulled his head further into his turned-up collar and struck one foot against the other.

"I don't own the tram," he replied. "Get on, if you like. But they don't hire your kind at my place of work. Have you a *propyska?*"

"No," said Andriy, deeply hurt by the phrase "your kind."

"And a *dovidka* (certificate on social background)? Do you have that?"

"No."

"Then don't waste your time. They won't hire you."

"Perhaps you know of another place where they would?" persisted Andriy, feeling as if a great burden had suddenly come down on his shoulders.

The man shrugged and turned away.

Another man, however, piped up, "We'd need three cities the size of Kharkiv to be able to register and employ all of you looking for shelter these days. Perhaps even three cities this size would not be enough!"

Again, the reference to "all of you" felt like a slap in the face. Andriy stepped out of the line and went dejectedly on his way. He walked to the next tram stop and again approached people and asked about work. Again he heard the same phrases in response—"people like you," "certificate of social background," "*propyska....*"

The phrase "people like you" was humiliating and depressing, and Andriy felt the rumblings of protest rising up within him. He had no desire to be lumped together with the people out there with their hands outstretched, those walking nightmares, those emaciated skeletons with swollen bellies who walked the streets until they either fell to their final sleep or propped themselves up to die against one or another gate in the city.

"No!" Andriy thought. "I want to face life head-on and win!"

Bursting with people, trams rolled swiftly by, their bells jingling. The streets were full of people hurrying in all directions. Shadowy figures of the starving began to appear, more and more of them, as if rising from the bowels of the earth. Andriy kept moving, from one tram stop to another, questioning passersby, but to no avail. They spoke as if in one voice, always mentioning the same documents, the ones Andriy did not have.

As the morning drew on and fewer and fewer people came to the tram stops, Andriy's hopes began to wane. Was it possible that he would not be able to find even the meanest of menial jobs or the hardest of difficult jobs in this city? Just as he was about to give up, along came a young man, who gave him his first glimmer of hope.

"A job, you say?" said the young man, repeating Andriy's question and scratching his head. "Who the devil knows! Maybe you should come with me. Our foreman is a really good egg. He's hired more than one like you. Maybe he'll hire you too! You are without documents?"

"Yes, without."

"Well then, follow me. I'll have a talk with our foreman. You see, ours is a really lousy job—we dig holes under the pavement—and we have a f . . . (he added an expletive) production quota. Not many manage to work at the pace they set. True, the quotas for juveniles are reduced, and there are about 10 youngsters working with us. Their contribution is rather negligible, but still . . . ."

"Oh, if they would just hire me!" cried Andriy fervently. "I'd work as hard and as fast as any adult!"

"Oh well!" retorted the young man, getting angry. "If you are so zealous, then go to hell! He's going to work like an adult! That would give them an excuse to raise the adult quota even more. Get lost!" And he quickly moved ahead, paying no attention to Andriy's apologies and pleas. He just walked on, cursing and spitting angrily.

Andriy let him walk ahead about ten paces and then resolutely followed.

"If he won't speak to the foreman, well then I will myself," he thought. "All I have to do is find out where this place is."

They continued walking in this way for about a quarter of an hour. Finally they came to a big square, riddled with deep holes. In one corner stood a hut. A long line of workers stood in front of it. Those who had already signed in stood off to one side, alone or in small groups, talking or smoking.

"*Diad'ku*, who is the foreman here?" Andriy asked, stepping up to a worker who was standing by himself off to one side.

Scrutinizing him, the man responded reluctantly, "There he is, the one in the grey hat."

Summoning his courage, Andriy went up to the man, and addressed him respectfully, "Comrade Foreman, I was told you hire people without documents here. I do not have a *dovidka*. I've come from an orphanage."

The man turned his unfriendly grey eyes on Andriy, taking his time to respond. Slowly he pulled off his warm gloves and reached into his pocket for cigarettes. Nothing about his demeanor betrayed that he was the "good egg" that the young man had talked about, and Andriy even thought that perhaps he had been sent to the wrong person.

"Umm . . . well!" he finally let slip through gritted teeth, rolling a cigarette. "Hire someone who has no documents, you say? Oh yes, there was a man like that. He was still working here just yesterday, but no longer. He's been taken away. Imagine giving 'contras' like you government jobs. You vipers refuse to enter into state collective farms, and come to the city to find shelter?"

Savoring the sound of his own voice, the foreman wanted to get a rise out of Andriy. And he succeeded.

"Why don't *you* go live on a collective farm?" retorted Andriy, standing up even straighter as he spoke. "Why are *you* working in the city?"

"Close your trap before . . . ."

"I haven't got a trap. I have a mouth!" Andriy shouted back, clenching his fists. "If you don't want to hire me, then don't. But don't dare to insult me!"

The foreman reached for the strap dangling from his neck and raised the whistle that hung from it to his mouth. But, something unexpected happened. The young man whom Andriy had followed to this workplace stepped up to the man and grabbed him by the elbow. He drew him aside and whispered something in his ear. The foreman changed visibly. He dropped his whistle. Fear registered in his beady eyes.

"Umm . . . well!" he said, turning to Andriy, struggling to set his face into more friendly contours. "Understand, little tyke—it's forbidden. I don't make the orders here. The work here is hard, and only for adults. You could get badly hurt. No, no. This is not for you. It'll be better for you to go to an orphanage," he said, giving a thumb's up sign. "You'll have your own bed and a blanket. You'll be able to go to school. There will be all sorts of extra benefits. You won't have to work hard, only some light chores."

"Oh, how well I know!" Andriy shot back. "I've told you from the very beginning that I have come from an orphanage."

Confused, the man said, "What, you didn't like it? It wasn't good?"

"Oh, it was good all right," said Andriy, most seriously. "May you and your children have as good a life as that to the end of your days."

He left without waiting for a reply.

A bell rang and the workers took up their posts. On his way out, Andriy walked past two policemen standing near the hut.

The young man who had just intervened on his behalf called after him, "Hey, what's your-name? Wait up!"

Surprised, Andriy stopped.

"Take this!" He handed Andriy a green paper note, just barely suppressing a laugh. "The foreman asked me to give you this three-ruble note."

"For me?" said Andriy, taken aback. "What for?"

"I told the foreman that you are a member of the Hvozdyk Krapochka gang," he said, laughing.

"Who?"

"Hvozdyk Krapochka. Haven't you heard of him? He's the leader of a gang of *blats*. Reputedly, his gang includes one hundred of them. Last month, the police killed one of Krapochka's underlings and imprisoned two others. The gang retaliated by shooting police in broad daylight for about a week. They let the police know that the killing would continue until the two were released. And they were released. Those guys don't fool around. That's why the foreman got frightened."

"What? Me? A member of a gang of criminals! Me?" shouted Andriy. "Why?"

"I could punch you for that even though I am younger than you!"

"You're an idiot," retorted the lad good-naturedly. "I have just saved your skin! Didn't you see that the man was about to blow his whistle? He was going to summon the police. Had they come, it would have been all over for you. You'd disappear without a trace. Here, take the money. I've got to get back to work!"

"Tell your foreman to choke on it."

"You don't want it?"

"No."

The lad scratched his head and then burst out laughing, "Now you really will scare him to death. He'll be sure that you will take revenge."

"Let him think what he wants."

"You know, it's worth the three rubles. Indeed, let him think! Let him shake in his pants. He'll be frightened of his own shadow now. Getting on the wrong side of Krapochka's gang is a sure death sentence. You know, little tyke, I'd give you two rubles out of my own pocket, if I only had them! Well, goodbye!" And he left, waving the three-ruble note and laughing as he walked back.

After this incident, Andriy became bolder and more determined. He no longer approached people just at tram stops. He widened his search, walking up to all sorts of people on the street, at least those who seemed approachable and kind. Still, he had no luck. Most people told him they simply had no idea where he could find work. Others advised him to go to the Donbas and Kryvyj Rih region of Ukraine and apply for work in the mines there. They said that even in these times it was probably easiest to find work there. There were also those who would start lecturing Andriy, all the while scowling in anger. They would start out with, "there is no work here for people like you." Then they would pick up steam and go on: "The government had good reason to pass a law forbidding people to hire workers who don't have a *dovidka* or a *propyska*. Go join the collective farm like you're supposed to! If you don't want to, then die! People in cities need bread, not additional workers. The city is hungry, too."

While the people who lectured Andriy did not necessarily like the government, they still harbored a hostile attitude toward the farmers. They accused them of "sabotaging collective farm construction."

One such person spoke to Andriy with open hatred, saying, "If all of you people joined the collective farms, there would be bread and work for everybody. But no! You won't do it, preferring to die. And you don't allow us to live. Vermin!"

At that, Andriy lost his patience with the young man, perhaps three years older than him, and lashed out:

"Little do you know, you sniveling dunce! Why don't you go to the *kolhosp* (collective farm), and do that back-breaking work on the land from sunrise to sunset for the 200 grams of barley a day they'll dole out to you for your troubles. You would understand the farmers then! Our farmers working on these collective farms were the first people in the country whose bellies swelled up from malnourishment."

"Because they worked only half-heartedly!"

"Go and work better, then. See what *you* get for your trouble!"

This was all very discouraging. But now that he thought of it, Andriy really did not know what he was expecting of life at this time. He had eyes to see and a head to understand all that was happening around him. Still he stubbornly continued searching for the impossible.

He walked on, speaking to passersby less and less frequently. He continued to be on the lookout for places of work—workshops, sawmills, warehouses, and other places where hired employees worked. Sometimes he dropped in to ask if they needed an extra pair of hands. Some places turned him away in a more or less civilized manner. Others practically threw him back out into the street. All the while, the cold was piercing through his light clothes, and hunger was gnawing at him and draining his strength. Now the sight of thousands of people like him brought a new and frightening thought, "I am one of them! Just as all the passersby had said." Still, something from within him protested, "No I am not! I am not starving! I will not stretch out my hands for alms!"

He was not sure how much ground he had covered that day, but he knew it was a lot. His feet began to give way beneath him. Andriy boarded the first tram he saw and sat down to ride and rest. He had no idea where he was going, but he didn't care. He was happy that there was room to sit down and give his feet a rest. Unfortunately, this pleasant ride lasted only about half an hour.

"Red Army Square!" the conductor called out in Russian. "Everybody out!"

Andriy at once regretted having spent the money Savchenko had given him to pay for the fare to the city center. He quickly realized that there was no hope of finding a job here. The tall office buildings that surrounded him probably had no need for manual workers, especially not ones without documents. The glass and concrete were cold and hard like the hearts of people here.

Was it just his imagination or were the people here, in the

center of town, really even more callous and less hospitable than those he had met out in the peripheries? Perhaps they weren't, but Andriy no longer had the heart to face people's sneers by asking for work. He walked on, trying only to find a route that would place the wind at his back. He had concluded that he would not find work that day. He would go back to the Savchenkos. The old man had said he should come back, but only after nightfall. At that thought, Andriy got a real jolt. In his haste to leave that morning, he had not taken note of the address of the school. What an idiot! A real idiot! What was he going to do now?

He looked around helplessly and saw that there was not even one other starving person on the streets of the city center. This frightened him even more. Though he desperately did not want to be considered a member of that group of people, when he found himself exclusively among people who surely did have a *propyska*, a *dovidka* and a job—with not even one of those shadowy figures around—he felt lonelier than ever. The "legal" city dwellers were all around, all hurrying somewhere. Clearly, they had somewhere to go. Each had a determined look on his or her face. None paid any attention to Andriy. All were indifferent.

He walked on, putting one foot ahead of the other with great difficulty. If only he could find a place to sit down for a bit. But there was nowhere to sit. He wanted to eat so badly he would gladly have chewed on his own fingertips. He had never ever been so very hungry before.

By twilight he had managed to walk far enough from the city center to enter a less urban neighborhood. Once again, he began seeing the tragic figures of the starving. Somehow, finding himself among them once again made him feel a bit better. At least he didn't feel so alone.

Walking along a rather quiet street, Andriy saw a scene that was strange even in these unusual times: a man was carrying two huge bundles over one shoulder while holding on to two small children with his left hand, and supporting a woman by the waist with his right. She leaned on him as if onto a crutch. The man's bundles kept falling down on the children's heads, getting in their way and making them cry. The woman cried out in pain at almost every step and struggled to keep from falling. Even though he was walking at a slow pace himself, it did not take Andriy a long time to catch up with this miserable group.

"*Diad'ku* Klym!" Andriy shouted in surprise, recognizing a neighbor from his village.

"Yakym's Andriy!" cried out the man in response, completely taken aback. "How terrible you look! Only your eyes still gleam."

"You think you look better than me? But what is wrong with *Titka* Yavdonia?"

As they talked, the woman leaned against the wall and was attempting to wipe perspiration off her forehead with her grimy hand.

"She was trampled by a crowd when trying to buy 'commercial bread.'[10] May these people never find any peace!" cursed Klym in response. Andriy did not know whether the curse was meant for those who had trampled his wife or for the officials responsible for the policies that had led to the melee.

"Help us, Andriy, help us to the tram stop."

Yavdonia sighed and cried out in pain and began slipping down the wall. She would have fallen had her husband not caught her.

"I can't, Klymtsiu darling!" she moaned, breathing with difficulty. "I can't! Leave me here. Go with the children."

"Stop talking nonsense!" he said in a tone at once imploring and reproachful. "What are you without us, and we without you? We'd perish, all of us! Don't be stubborn, Yavdonia. I'll find a bench on the train for you to lie on. You'll be comfortable, you'll see!"

"It might be better, *diad'ku,* to take her to the hospital," advised Andriy.

"We've been there already," replied the man angrily. "'No room,' they said. 'Go to your regional hospital!' Help us, Andriy, won't you?"

Andriy glanced at the enormous bundles and thought that he was too tired and too hungry to lift them.

"They're light," said Klym, guessing his thoughts. "Two down comforters, a sheepskin coat, and a piece of sackcloth—that's all."

But even with Andriy's help, things did not get much better. Andriy carried the bundles. Klym carried his wife, and told the children to walk alongside and hold on to his coattails. But Yavdonia was a tall and boney woman, and it wasn't easy to carry her, while the children—they were only three and four years old—cried and complained all of the time, and kept falling behind. As a result, they all had to stop every few steps, set Yavdonia down on the bundles, and go and get the children.

---

[10] Bread available for sale to anyone who could afford to pay the 3 rubles per loaf.

During one of these pauses, Klym began talking about his adventures. Before de*kurkul*ization, he had squirreled away some things, having a premonition that things were going badly in the country and that there would come a time when they would not have their own roof over their heads. He had fled the village back in early spring. Coming to Kharkiv, he had carved a mud hut in the earth for the family to live in just outside the city, and was lucky enough to find a job as a loader at the railroad station. All too soon, however, they were "exposed" as illegal residents, and Klym was fired. Some time later, the police raided their neighborhood, ordered all the huts filled, and dispersed everyone. Klym and his family have been wandering the city's streets since, carrying their "home" on their backs, like snails. At night, they would find some quiet corner, spread out the blankets and comforters and sleep. Klym would go and take his place in line for "commercial bread." In the morning, Yavdonia would arrive to take his place in line, while he went back to the children. It was not clear how things would unfold from here on, but while working at the station, Klym got to know a person who managed to get him train tickets to the Donbas. They were scheduled to leave on the 10:00 PM train.

"Maybe you should come with us?" said Klym.

"Where would I get money for a ticket?" replied Andriy glumly.

"Even if you had any, money wouldn't help you one bit. People have been standing in line for weeks to purchase tickets and have come away with nothing. You should try 'riding rabbit' as we call it. If not for my wife and children, I would have certainly done so and I'd have been in the Donbas ages ago! I'd grab hold of something, or crawl onto some ledge or other, and away we go! Only one percent of the passengers on trains these days actually have tickets. The rest 'ride rabbit.'"

"Oh yes," said his wife bitterly. "I am sure that they pick these 'rabbits' up by the dozen at every station—all frozen stiff!"

"Yes," Klym replied. "But many more dead—several hundred!—are carted off the city's streets each morning. Few have down comforters like us."

Talking in this way, they finally arrived at the tram stop. Klym begged Andriy to stay with them and help them to the station. Again he tried to talk him into coming with them to the Donbas.

"It's still easier for people like us to get jobs there," he said. "People are not that eager to work in the mines."

"They're not that eager because there is no certainty that, once they go down, they will ever come back up to see the light of day again," spoke up Yavdonia bitterly.

Andriy did not find this a convincing argument. He thought that these days it might be easier to survive underground in the mines than above ground here.

They had to let a few trams go by because bundles as large as theirs were not allowed on a tram. But one came along whose driver was more understanding. He turned a blind eye to the baggage and let them board. Klym paid Andriy's fare, and they were finally on their way to their destination, Kharkiv's Balashivska Station. Only the "cleaner" public was allowed access to the central station; the starving had to be satisfied with the side station.

The distance between the tram stop and the station was quite long. As they were passing a kiosk selling beer, Klym decided to buy some. He asked for three mugs of the warm beverage, one for Andriy.

"Ah, things would be really fine if there was a slice of bread and some pickled herring to go with this beer," he said. "But, as there is none, we'll just have to enjoy the drink all by itself. It will surely warm us up a bit. The Armenians have a saying about life under the Soviets—'Eat water. Drink water.'"

The children also begged for some of the warm liquid. They took a sip, spat it out, wiped their mouths off, and clamored for more.

The journey took on a more comic and happier, if also more catastrophic character. The warm beer, on empty stomachs, was a powerful intoxicant. They no longer walked along, but rather weaved, inscribing strange curlicues along the sidewalk as they went. All the while, Yavdonia, let out whimpers of pain, interspersed with shouts and curses.

The railroad station was packed. It was smelly, heavy with cigarette smoke, and filled with a cacophony of voices. People lined up in front of an obviously closed ticket agent's office. A cardboard sign on its window announced: "No tickets." Some wit had scribbled in, "without a *khabar* (bribe)". It was common knowledge that two or three people a day actually did manage to buy tickets here after bribing one of the agents. So people continued to line up, to argue, and to demand to be served. They had more arguments with the agent who was honest and who would not take bribes than with the ones who did.

The room was only dimly lit by a yellowish light which, when mixed with the smoke in the room, made everybody appear blackish. People were half-lying down, half-sitting on the dirty ground, wet from the snow others had tracked in on their shoes. Any change in place meant climbing over numbers of people. Observing the scene, Andriy had the feeling that he had fallen into a basket brimming over with live crabs. Only this was worse, for crabs did not have voices and did not smoke the vile cigarettes rolled from ordinary newspaper and *makhorka* (cheap, strong and foul-smelling tobacco made of tobacco plant stems).

Andriy's party managed to push their way only a short distance into the room when they had to stop. People were sitting so tightly packed that it would be difficult to squeeze even a nail in between them. To get a spot, you had to crawl into the crowd and pry a space open for yourself. Yavdonia cried out in pain again, the children started crying again, and Klym had to quiet everybody down with promises of comfortable benches in a warm train, of bread aplenty in the Donbas when they finally got there, and a variety of other "pears from willow trees."

People were talking all around them, and nothing they said was too encouraging. Listening in, Andriy quickly picked up that, more often than not, the trains that pull into the station are already full, and that they pause for only about five minutes at the station. Passengers with tickets wishing to board had no guarantee of being able to do so at this station. Many brave souls somehow figured out how to climb onto the roof of the station. From there, they would leap onto the train as it was pulling out. Andriy also learned that Klym was overly optimistic about the chances of "riding rabbit." All stations were manned by large contingents of militia, and their numbers were augmented with army units. Only passengers with tickets were allowed on the boarding platforms the length and breadth of the station. He might have found out a whole lot more had not the combination of the beer and exhaustion suddenly caught up with him and carried him off into a deep sleep.

The beer acted as a powerful drug. Andriy had difficulty waking even when he was being jostled from all sides. The crush of people pushed him into an upright position, and people were shouting right into his ears. Moments of clarity alternated with moments of renewed unconsciousness. He suddenly realized he was "riding rabbit" on the express train—well, not riding, but being pulled, his feet tied to the train and his head dangling and banging painfully—almost bursting—against the crossties supporting the rail tracks. Andriy twisted, turned, screamed, and finally regained consciousness from the cold. All around he heard a heavy drumming beat, curses, cries, threats, and a penetrating animal-like voice, screaming in Russian: "Leave! Disperse!"

One could hear shots fired at a distance, rising pandemonium, the quickening pace of a drumming beat, as if a train was gathering speed. Andriy got to his feet, totally confused.

"Wh-at? What's happening? What is going on here?" No one answered.

Andriy started running as well, catching a phrase here and there, which allowed him to start piecing together what was going on. Apparently a group of people had climbed to the roof of the station in anticipation of an approaching train, hoping to hop on. The militia had come in to clear the place and throw out those without tickets. The gunshots he had heard was the militia shooting at these "rabbits." Everybody had been thrown out of the waiting room and ordered not to come back.

Andriy felt his head, which was full of bumps, and discovered that his hat had fallen off. There was no way to go back and look for it. Anyway, how could one possibly find anything in that hell?

Days and nights can be short, like happiness, or long, like grief. To Andriy this night was endless . . . .

He joined a large group that was grudgingly walking away from the station and started listening to the conversations around him. The pessimists were saying that it was clear that nobody would be allowed back into the waiting room that night, and so it was better to look for a place to sleep elsewhere. The optimists, however, thought that all they had to do was to wait for the train to leave the station (the train Klym had managed to get tickets for), and then they would be able to come back.

"The devil himself knows what tricks they will be up to!" a clear male voice spoke up. "Sometimes they let you in. Sometimes they throw you out. One day they ask for tickets, the next day they ask for documents. Sometimes they command you to form a line. At other times, they scatter everybody, their sticks swinging. One can never know what to expect!"

Still, part of the group decided to wait. With nowhere to go, Andriy decided to wait as well. He was very hungry, and his stomach—irritated by the beer—was cramping badly, as if trying to turn itself inside out.

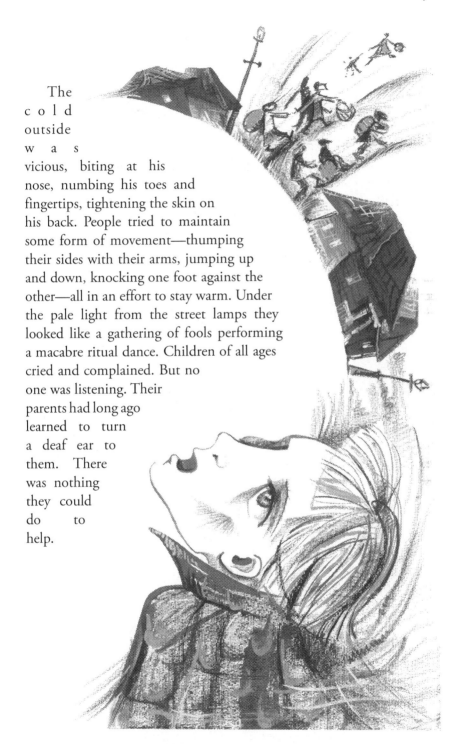

The
c o l d
outside
w a s
vicious, biting at his
nose, numbing his toes and
fingertips, tightening the skin on
his back. People tried to maintain
some form of movement—thumping
their sides with their arms, jumping up
and down, knocking one foot against the
other—all in an effort to stay warm. Under
the pale light from the street lamps they
looked like a gathering of fools performing
a macabre ritual dance. Children of all ages
cried and complained. But no
one was listening. Their
parents had long ago
learned to turn
a deaf ear to
them. There
was nothing
they could
do   to
help.

Andriy, too, ran in place, beat his arms against his sides, did squats. He took a piece of lining from his coat and put it on his bare head. This left his back even more exposed to the cold, and Andriy alternated between putting the cloth on his head and on his body in an effort to keep warm. Whatever he did, some part of his body—either his head or his back—was freezing.

They waited for two hours in the cold. Then they heard the thundering of an approaching train and the screeching of brakes and rails as the train came to a stop at the station. There was a great commotion, and the screams and whistles of the militia were heard for three blocks around. In five minutes, a bell sounded again, and the train rolled out of the station. The group Andriy was with did not wait long before they grabbed their parcels and hurried back to the station.

Andriy, who had nothing to carry, was one of the first to return to the waiting room. The militia was gone. The doors stood wide open. He jumped in and found a place in a corner farthest away from the door. Cuddling up, he looked around for Klym. Neither Klym nor any member of his family was around. They must have been lucky and boarded the train.

It was cold and drafty in the waiting room. It became warmer once the door was closed and people huddled together. But Andriy could not feel that warmth. His body seemed to radiate cold from inside. He started trembling all over, as if he had a fever.

Outside when he'd been trying to stay warm, his most fervent wish had been to curl up in a corner of the waiting room and sleep. Sleep would give him the rest he needed and allow him to forget the hunger eating at his insides and the disillusionment he was feeling with this city of his dreams. Now that he had the opportunity, sleep evaded him. All kinds of useless thoughts swam in his head. His stomach was growling, demanding food. It was about midnight when he finally fell asleep.

He dreamed of his mother. She was taking out a loaf of freshly-baked bread from their tiled oven back home. Andriy grabbed a knife, cut off a large chunk from the end, and began to chew. But what was this? Though just out of the oven, the bread was cold and did not have the usual mouth-watering aroma or the delicious taste of his mother's bread. He was just about to ask his mother why, when pandemonium broke out again all around him—screams, cries, and curses—waking him up with a jolt.

"Leave the premises! Disperse! Come on, come on! Faster!" a voice yelled in Russian.

One person started to plead, another to argue. Some started crying. Others cursed. Nothing helped. They had to move out. They moved slowly and unwillingly, but they moved. Andriy was the last one to leave. He was mad. So mad, he could no longer restrain himself. Passing a young militiaman at the door, he hissed at him, "Is there no plague that could wipe you out?! Do you so begrudge people this barn of a place, that you won't leave them here in peace?"

"Move along, move along," replied the youth peaceably. "Don't you understand? An order is an order!" And in a whisper, he added, "We'll see the train through in half and hour. Then you can come back."

What was news for Andriy was not news for the other people who were talking among themselves.

"They are sending our bread to Moscow again. They are chasing us out to make sure we don't catch them in the act."

"So it wasn't such a stupid person who made up that ditty: '*my own grain has become my bane*.'"

"Wasn't it enough to rob us of everything we had? Do they now have to chase us, like dogs, from one place to another!"

"Ah, this is the government's way of looking after us. They don't want us to salivate too much when we catch a whiff of our own grain whizzing by on these trains!"

"Hmm, I rather think they want to avoid our skin from spiking in anger," added another. "In Merefa, two prisoner transport trains bound for Siberia, jam-packed with people like herring in a barrel, were sidelined for two days to allow these grain trains speedy passage. Imagine the suffering of those people, their cries and their curses. It's so sad!"

"Who told you?"

"Nobody told me. I saw it with my own eyes. I was in Merefa just yesterday."

"Dear God! Our life is bitter and difficult. But when you look and listen, you realize that there are many in our country, who would envy even us, and with good reason."

"Yes, we're unhappy at being moved from place to place, but those unfortunate people would give a lot just to be able to walk freely."

"I heard that those prisoners are from Vovchiv. It seems people rebelled there. They killed the head of the village council and another regional

Communist official. The GPU[11] responded by raiding the town and executing the instigators on the spot. They then set fire to the village and hung a black flag over it.[12] Those who managed to survive were packed into wagons and—off to Siberia!"

"You think this is happening only in Vovchiv?" A young woman, with an infant swaddled in her arms, spoke up for the first time. "People everywhere are rebelling. Enough is enough!"

"Ah, if only it were true that people are rebelling everywhere!" said a newcomer, an older man in enormous patched felt boots. "Trouble is, it's not true. If everybody in this country rebelled, things would be different."

"Tired of living, are you, *diad'ku*, saying such things out loud?" piped up a person in the group. "One never knows who could be listening and . . . ."

"Yes!" replied the man, turning in the general direction of the last speaker. "If there is a Judas hiding among us, let him listen and run to the authorities and inform them. People are tired of this life! You call this living? In years gone by, stray dogs lived better than we do today."

"Keep talking like that and your life will surely get better!" called out a mocking voice.

"Naturally, talk alone won't make anything better," replied the man, without the slightest hint of rancor. "But if one were to really focus on doing something . . . . One hears of Committees of Self Defense being organized in one place or another, like the ones during the Revolution."

"So why are you still standing here? Quick! Run! They need people like you!" said the same mocking voice.

"They need all kinds of people!" the man snapped back. "In 1921, when the Soviets came to the villages to requisition food, women grabbed poker irons and attacked the *Chervona Mitla* (Red Broom) brigades, while children hurled stones and clods of earth at them. The *Chervona Mitla* brigades fled like there was no tomorrow! Superior arms could not withstand that popular uprising, armed only with pitchforks, scythes, and women's kitchen tools.

---

[11] Precursors of the KGB, the Soviet secret police.

[12] This was not an uncommon sight in Ukraine in the 1930s after villages had been completely "vanquished."

"They didn't have good weapons back in those days! Only rifles without cartridges and whips! Try to fight with poker irons now!"

"Of course!" the man snapped back. "Today we should simply die without a fight. Like the old saying: 'Don't waste your energy, buddy, just let yourself sink down to the bottom.' We are dying more passively than lambs being led to slaughter."

Andriy was hanging on to every word, but the conversation ended there. Famished people, forced to keep moving in order not to freeze and die of the cold are not so keen on long discussions. As it turned out, they had to keep moving for much longer than the half hour the militiaman had promised.

Finally the train arrived. It did not even stop at the station, only rolled through at a reduced speed, and then sped noisily on. This time, however, nobody even bothered to speculate about what its cargo was—prisoners to Siberia or grain to Russia. The main concern was getting back to the waiting room as quickly as possible and finding the best possible spot to rest and thaw out.

Andriy again managed to be the first one back. The old man in the patched felt boots was right behind him. They both hurried to the far corner of the room, and sat down next to each other.

"Well, we're back home again," quipped the man and reached for his tobacco.

"Have you been here long?" asked Andriy.

"Hmm, depends what you mean by long. I've probably been here three weeks."

"Always in quest of a ticket?"

"Don't be silly, what ticket?" he sighed, and began to roll a cigarette. "I come here at night to sleep. By day, I wander about the city."

"Looking for a job?"

"Yes, I always look around. Mostly, though, I spend my time wheeling and dealing. I stand in lines at the bazaars, purchase goods and then resell them at a profit. Wherever there are people—there, too, am I."

Though the light in the waiting room was dim, Andriy could make out that his new acquaintance had an intelligent face and dark questioning eyes.

"How do you do this wheeling and dealing?" Andriy asked.

"Hmm . . . in various ways. For example, yesterday, I stood in a line through the night and finally was able to purchase a pair of ladies' rubber boots. I sold them on the black market, bought a kilo of bread and pocketed the change. I buy whatever is available—candy, chocolates, herring—right there at the bazaar, buying from one person and selling to another. I come here at night to sleep, first because I do not have a *propyska*, but also because it's somehow comforting to be with other people. Though they complain interminably and quarrel amongst themselves, they are still trying. They haven't given up like those others who stand on the streets with outstretched hands, dying off like flies. How far our people have fallen! Had I not seen this with my own eyes, I would never have believed it!" He blew out some smoke and shut his eyes.

"*Diad'ku*, Andriy said, moving closer to the man, "you said something about some committees. Is it true?"

The old man lifted his head and gazed at Andriy attentively.

"What's it to you?"

"Well," replied Andriy, drawing up even closer. "If I knew how to find my way to one . . . ."

"You're too young!" said the old man, cutting him off.

"Not too young to die of hunger, though, am I?" Andriy fired back angrily. "Didn't you say that they needed all kinds of people there?"

"But that's just it. People are needed there, not here!" he explained, looking intently into Andriy's face to see if he was beginning to understand. "The people who have come here have renounced everything in the hope of finding a piece of bread. There are many people in the villages holding onto their ancestral lands with pincer-like grips. They fight for this land with every last bit of strength and sinew. They even die for it if they have to. But when they die, they die in their own homes and on their own lands. These are the people who are the backbone of the committees. They are the ones who raid the trains that are carrying grain out of the country, derail them, and haul the grain out, sack by sack. They are the ones who are publishing and disseminating leaflets, educating people about what is going on. They're the ones who encourage people to organize and rise up in protest, to revolt."

"Really?" asked Andriy, amazed and moved.

"You haven't heard? Go to Izium. Many such things are happening there."

"Izium? But I'm from the Okhtyrka area. That's in the opposite direction."

"There are people still living there, and the situation is just as bad as everywhere else."

The man gazed long and intently into Andriy's face, as if wanting to see right through him.

"Well, all right, lad!" he said finally, obviously satisfied with what he saw. "Now let's get some sleep. I'll try to doze off for about an hour. Then I'll get up and make my way into town in the hopes of sniffing out some business. You can come with me, if you like. I'll show you how this wheeling and dealing is done."

He lay down, curled up into a ball, covered his eyes with an old sheepskin hat, and placed his arm under his head for support. Andriy tried to sleep as well, but he was so excited that he knew he would find it difficult.

However, neither of them was to get any sleep that night. No sooner had they settled down, when all hell broke loose again. Shots were fired outside. They were followed by loud screams. The door to the waiting room suddenly flew open, and two shabby figures jumped into the room. They made their way quickly to the door on the opposite side of the room, clambering over bodies in various stages of repose. Close behind them, five militiamen were giving chase, with ready rifles. They, too, scrambled towards the door, but their rifles got in their way, slowing down their progress. By the time they reached the door, the men had disappeared into the night. Frustrated, the militiamen returned to take out their anger on the unfortunate people in the room.

"Clear out!" they yelled. "Out! Every one of you, out! We're locking this place up till morning! Move!"

Again people begged, argued, and cursed. Somewhere a child cried out, and then sobbed convulsively, as it was being pushed and pulled by the throng. The scene was appalling. The militiamen remained unmoved, intent on clearing out the room. They used the butts of their rifles to push and prod people out the door and into the street.

With two or three hundred people inside, clearing the room took a while. The old man turned to Andriy, and said, "Well, I guess that's it for tonight. Better head into town now and start looking for a promising queue to line up on."

"I've no reason to stand in line. I haven't got a *kopijka* (penny) to my name to buy anything with," Andriy answered, suddenly feeling really sleepy.

"Don't worry, I'll lend you a few. Stay near me and we'll take our places in line together. We'll each buy a kilogram of bread for 3 *rubles*, eat one and sell one at the market for 7 *rubles*. That way, we'll make 50 *kopijkas* profit each. Not a bad gain on top of a full stomach!"

While the prospect of profit did not make a great impression on Andriy, the mere thought of having half a kilogram of bread to eat in one sitting was enough to unleash all the hungry demons in his stomach, and he began salivating. His body started to shake from hunger and exhaustion. He felt his anger rising at the militiamen's cruel and arbitrary display of power. There they were mercilessly shoving the whole crowd, Andriy among them, into the cold, and nobody could do anything to stop them. Again, Andriy was not able to contain himself. Squeezing through the door, he suddenly let his fury fly into the enraged snout of one of these keepers of law and order, "Sic'm, you little bloodhounds! Bite them!"

The officer's eyes widened in surprise and his mouth dropped open at this unexpected show of arrogance. Realizing that his actions would certainly not go unchallenged, Andriy quickly, but in a most dignified manner, moved past the man, purposely taking the longest possible strides.

"Halt! Halt! Come back here!" he heard behind him. The words, shouted in Russian, were a signal for Andriy to take off! He lunged forward and cut into the crowd.

"Hold him! Hold him! Stop! I'm shooting!" came more shouts from behind him.

Nobody in the crowd would ever think of handing Andriy over to the militia. But they did unwittingly slow Andriy's escape, as frightened people jumped in every direction. Andriy had to elbow his way through, pushing people aside, even knocking one person down, in his haste to get away. In so doing, he cut such a wide swath behind him that it would have been easy for a horse-drawn cart to follow. Down this path, leopard-like, lunged the officer, shouting, "Halt! Halt! I'm firing!" He fired two shots into the air. Andriy was in real danger now, for he was out of the safety of the crowd and an open target.

"Halt or I'll shoot!" warned the officer as he was catching up to Andriy.

The situation was desperate. Quickly, without much thought, Andriy decided on a bold step, one that he had tried many times and perfected as a young boy in fights with the neighborhood kids. He spun around sharply, now facing the militiaman, and stuck out his foot to trip him up. The move had the desired effect. Taken by surprise, the officer, unable to stop, went sprawling. The revolver shot out wildly, the bullet sped forward, skimming the top of the sidewalk.

Andriy took off. He ran without thought to direction, heard nothing but the sound of whistles blowing behind him and the sound of his own steps. He knew for certain, however, that the militia would give chase. He ran on, passing the beer-seller's kiosk—now closed—a large corner building, a small narrow street on the left . . . All were quickly left behind as he ran. Another street . . . another corner building . . . a very narrow street . . . a solitary tree . . . all loomed ahead of him and then remained behind as he ran past them. More buildings, more narrow streets, yet another corner building—a larger one this time, and a tall wooden fence behind it. Without as much as a thought, Andriy jumped up, caught hold of the spikes of the fence and catapulted his body over the fence and to the other side with the agility of a cat. He found himself in an urban courtyard. Apart from the main building, there was a crooked little house with a shed and a latrine next to it. The windows were all dark, the shutters tightly shut.

Bending over, Andriy put his ear to the fence. The sound of running feet! Their boots rang on the frozen ground, echoing all around. Not a second to waste! They might guess that he had jumped over the fence. They might even have seen him do it!

He plunged further into the courtyard, jumped over another fence—a lower one this time, and found himself in another courtyard, one that led to the other side of the neighborhood. Again, he saw two buildings, two woodsheds and a latrine. Andriy inched his way stealthily underneath the windows, let himself out through a gate in the fence, stepped out into the street, looked around, and breathed a deep sigh of relief: the street was completely empty!

Closing the gate carefully behind himself, he walked on as quickly as he could. By now Andriy had completely forgotten that he was hungry and tired. He was hot from running and could feel drops of perspiration rolling down his back. He was very thirsty.

Luckily, not far away, he happened on a public water tap. The faucet was broken and water was trickling down in a thin stream, freezing into a treacherous sheet of ice below the tap. At the risk of slipping and breaking his neck, Andriy crawled up to the spout, positioned his lip under it, and drank greedily.

Finally, he had his fill. He slid back down to the ground. Wiping his sweaty forehead with the wet palm of his hand, he slid back down to the sidewalk. The cold wind licked his moist face and sweat-drenched back. His stomach, heavy with all the cold water, began protesting. Andriy's whole body started to shake uncontrollably. Where to go? Where to find some warmth? Where to rest for even just one hour?

Suddenly, despair overcame him. Morbid indifference enveloped him. He wanted to collapse on this very spot and close his eyes for eternity. How good it was to stretch out here and not think about anything. Let the cold suck at his heart, let the frost eat right into his bones: he did not care: he would ignore it. Then he thought again about the mysterious old man. Dear God, how could he have strayed so far away from him? What an idiot he was! Twice now he had encountered good and well-intentioned people, and twice he had stupidly lost them.

The very thought of the old man, however, steered Andriy's thoughts in a different direction.

"I must return to the village," he told himself. This decision cheered him up immediately.

Truly, why continue roaming the streets in this unfamiliar city when he has his family home in the village. He will go back, gather twigs and leaves and use them to light a fire, then climb onto the hearth and rest and sleep to his heart's content. Nobody will throw him out from there several times a night. After resting, he will find a way to get food. He will set a net to snare a crow or a trap for a rabbit, and try his luck at fishing in the river. But here? What was he to do? In a day and a half, he had not seen even one small bird. He saw only concrete, high fences, starving people, and strangers who did not care a whit about him. On the other hand, in the village everybody knows one another. And who knows if in Hrun', his native village, people are not already organizing themselves into a Committee of Self Defense. People knew him there, and would let him also join. And if such a committee does not exist already, Andriy would talk with some of the sensible farmers there and encourage them to follow the example of the people of Izium. That old man was right. People everywhere face the same problems as people in Izium.

So—home! Soon it will be daylight, and he will ask for directions and be on his way. Right now, however, he must keep on walking in spite of his weariness. He must overcome the temptation to sit down and rest. For if he sits down now he will never get up again.

And so he walked wherever his eyes led him. He now had a clear goal and a vague, but warm, sense of hope. His life was taking on meaning again, the suffering he had been through had not been in vain. This new wave of enthusiasm brought renewed energy to his feeble body, and he walked with greater certainty. Too bad he could not begin the journey straightaway. But day was not far off—another three or four hours, and the sun would come up.

Three or four hours . . . . How short a time and how interminably long.

3

Night was falling. The cold was again pressing from all directions. The wind, laced with sand and needles of icy snow, whipped Andriy's face and chilled his bare hands until they burned. Barely able to put one foot ahead of the other, Andriy continued roaming the streets of some Kharkiv suburb.

Strange, but all day long he was not able to get clear directions to Okhtyrka. He felt as if he were trapped in a hopeless and accursed labyrinth with no exit. Most people responded to his query with a straightforward, "I don't know." Others didn't bother to respond at all. Instead, they hunched over a bit more and kept on walking. Those who knew the way gave Andriy complicated and essentially useless directions. They'd say, "Well, first walk along that street there, then turn right, take tram number such and such to stop such and such, then transfer to tram number such and such, and go to . . ." and so on. Andriy couldn't take a tram. He had no money. And his head was so dull from hunger and fatigue that he couldn't retain the names of the streets or keep the rest of the directions straight either. All this gave him the impression that it was impossible to get out of this spellbound city. Taking a train would have been the easiest and most direct way, as one passerby told him, as he gave him directions to the train station. Andriy sighed and continued on his way.

Andriy managed to keep his spirits from flagging for the first half of the day. By the afternoon, however, he could feel that something strange was happening to him. His body was very hot and he desperately wanted something to drink. Looking around for a pile of snow, he grabbed a handful, wiped off the crust of dirt from the top, and sucked on it. His stomach immediately began to cramp from the cold, his legs began to tremble and buckle under him, and his lips became so numb he could hardly move them. He started to cough, and his eyes began to sting, so Andriy shut them for a few seconds. When he reopened them, everything—the buildings, the light posts, and the people on the street all took on strange forms, quivering and distending, as if they were images drawn on rippling water.

His appearance seemed to elicit sympathy, for several people pressed a few coins into his hand, though he did not have his hand out. His fingers closed on the coins automatically, without his being aware of what he was doing. Nor did he count them. In the state he was in it did not even occur to him that he might now have enough money to take a tram. His thoughts focused doggedly on finding the way out of Kharkiv in the direction of Okhtyrka. He didn't need trams now.

Andriy knew that Kharkiv was situated southeast of Okhtyrka. Okhtyrka, therefore, had to be northwest of Kharkiv. This was the only thing he knew with complete certainty. Had

he been able to find an open field, he would have been able to orient himself quickly by looking at the sun's position in the sky. But here in the city, the sun seemed to be playing hide-and-seek, and not follow a straight path. In the city it did not shine so brightly either, but seemed to hide itself in the hazy dullness of the sky. When it did appear, it seemed to pop out for a brief second from every possible direction—from the right, the left, straight up ahead, or from behind him. It was as if the sun was teasing him. Still, it did not bring any cheer, and it did not shine. It looked exhausted and pale, as if it were a ball of white porcelain. It peered out from above—a colorless matte orb—and then concealed itself again. Finally, at the end of the day it disappeared from view without the least bit of protest.

No longer asking anybody anything, Andriy walked on. Stubbornly he willed his feet to move forward. It took superhuman effort to keep walking and not sit down on some enticing snow-swept knoll that beckoned to him from in-between buildings and from comfortable-looking perches in front of gates. In this half-conscious state he passed, with complete indifference, hundreds of other unfortunate people just like him. What kept him going—the rock of his salvation—was the thought: "Go home! Go home!"

Yes, home! But before he could continue, he needed to warm up and get some rest. He'd have to beg his way into some house, not even to spend the night, but just to sit at the hearth for a short while and thaw out his frozen hands and body. While there, he would also try again to get some clear directions.

Should he knock on that door there? No, perhaps not . . . . That one, too, looked so . . . . Perhaps that door across the street? Maybe it would be best to ask for some shelter in that white house over there. Andriy passed one gate after another, unable to gather up enough courage to walk up and knock. He did not like to trouble strangers or to ask for anybody's help. It was not his way.

Finally he knew he could walk no further. If he did not rest, he would fall down and never get up again. In a wave of despair, he knocked on the nearest door. He knocked with all his strength, persistently and hard. He waited a moment, catching his breath, and knocked again. Nobody answered. Perhaps nobody was home? Perhaps they did not hear?

Nonsense, somebody was in. He saw a light through the cracks in the windows. Blinded by a kind of rage, Andriy hammered on the door. His knock was a wail of desperation, "Save me! I'm dying!!!"

Suddenly, the door flew open and a woman appeared. Taken by surprise, Andriy stood silent, dumbfounded, incapable of blurting out even one word.

"Hey, hothead! Knocking down the door, are you?" a woman shouted. "You've frightened the children to death! Thought there might be a fire somewhere, but it's only another beggar! As if we have nothing better to do all day than answer the door constantly!" she said, cursing.

"I . . . ," started Andriy timidly.

But the enraged woman would not let him finish.

"We have nothing!" she screamed. "We are hungry too. Get away from here because if I grab this piece of wood, I will break your legs with it!" And she slammed the door angrily.

"Who was it? Who was at the door?" Andriy heard a male voice ask from inside the house.

"Who else?" she replied, with anger in her voice. "Another beggar! And what a brazen one! Give me! Give me! He almost broke down the door. May they never find any good in the world!"

Andriy stood, dumbstruck by such disdain directed at him. He had never in his life experienced such humiliation. He—a beggar! He, the son of proud and dignified landowners, who considered borrowing from a neighbor—let along asking for something—as shameful, had now become a "beggar." At least that's how people must see him: the coins they had pressed into his hands were evidence of this. People gave him charity, and he had accepted it.

A beggar! A beggar! The coins in his pocket suddenly felt heavy and hot. They burned with the shaming he had just been subjected to. Andriy gathered up the coins and flung them to the pavement in disgust. He leaned against a light post and sighed deeply. He resigned himself to the thought that he would not find a way out today. And tomorrow—well, tomorrow would be too late. He would no longer be alive by tomorrow, but a boney skeleton in the street, a silvery filament of frost covering his body—a homeless and nameless beggar.

> *"Perhaps I shall not live to see*
> *The home that was so dear to me . . . .* [13] [14]

The words burst out of him, unbidden, from deep within. Surprised, he stopped in his tracks, touched to the core. Unexpectedly his thirsty lips had uttered words from a miracle-working source. He delighted in them and went back to wade more deeply into those healing waters.

> *". . . My gloomy day then passes by;*
> *Again the sky grows dark;*
> *And the strange mower above my head*
> *Again emerges stark,*
> *Bearing his dull, old scythe along . . .*
> *Soon silently he'll mow me—*
> *Winds will erase my slightest trace,*
> *With nothing left to show me."* [15]
> *God, this was about him, Andriy! Precisely about him.*
> *"But once it was my lot, on distant shores,*
> *To weep because I never had possessed*
> *That refuge sure, a home to call my own."* [16]

Suddenly, he stepped away from the lamppost, spread his arms out and deliriously cried out:

> *"Where art thou, Destiny, ah where?*
> *My soul is stirred by none!*
> *If Thou begrudgest me fair fate,*
> *Lord, send a ruthless one!*
> *Let me not sleep when I should wake,*
> *Do not permit my heart to lie*

---

[13]   Andriy recites many fragments of poems in this chapter. All of them are from Shevchenko's, monumental compilation, *The Kobzar*. The translations into English are taken from Andrusyshyn, C.H. and Kirkconnell, Watson, *The Poetical Works of Taras Shevchenko: The Kobzar*. (Toronto: University of Toronto Press, 1964.). See endnotes for the chapter for transliterated Ukrainian version of Shevchenko's poems cited in this chapter.

[14]   *"Zarosly shliakhy ternamy"* ("The Roads are Overgrown with Thorns"); Andrusyshyn et al., p. 438.

[15]   *"Slipyj"* ("The Blind Man"); Andrusyshyn et al., p. 194.

[16]   *"Dobro, u koho ye, Hospody"* ("Would that the headman's axe..."); Andrusyshyn et al., p. 365.

> *A rotten log that men forsake*
> *And leave in fetid infamy;*
> *But on me let fierce fervor fall*
> *To love all people all my days,*
> *Or let me cast a curse on all*
> *And set the torpid world ablaze!"*[17]

"Set ablaze! Set ablaze!" he screamed shrilly, and pounded with all his might on the very door he had been so coldly turned away from. "Set afire! So that everything would go to hell with the smoke!"

He did not wait to see if anyone would open the door. He continued walking down the street, feeling inexpressible happiness that his depression, despair and pain had at long last poured out of him in all their unfathomed depth. He could never have found the words to express as accurately all he was feeling, but he didn't have to. Someone had expressed it all for him—someone who had lived, suffered and endured many years earlier. That someone had foreseen Ukraine's (and Andriy's) fate and he was now extending a hand of support from the other world. Andriy continued reciting, resurrecting the words from the dry pages of a book he had memorized as a child, and giving them his own voice.

> *"Ukraine, alas, has fall'n asleep,*
> *Is overgrown with weeds*
> *And covered deep with slimy mould;*
> *It fails from noble deeds.*
> *Its heart decays in filthy mire*
> *And vipers are allowed*
> *Into its hollows cool to creep . . ."*[18]

"Yes, that's true!" he added. "It has fallen asleep, and is falling into eternal sleep right here, on the streets!"

A passersby avoided him, hugging the walls and giving him a wide berth as he passed. Paying no attention to anyone or anything, Andriy continued to scream and shout as he wended his way down the street:

---

[17]   *"Mynayut' dni, mynayut' nochi,"* ("The days pass by, the nights flit away"); Andrusyshyn et al., p. 268.

[18]   *"Chyhyryn,"*; Andrusyshyn et al., p. 151.

"Thus, in her struggle, our Ukraine
Reached the last climax of pure pain!"[19]

He paused for a moment in front of a mound, covered with one piece of tarpaulin, from under which a child's feet were sticking out, and this reminded him immediately of the lines:

". . . And there, by the hedge,
A child with swoll'n belly its pangs to allege
Is dying of hunger . . ."[20]

"A child!" he cried out. "Not one child but thousands! Thousands of children, large and small are wandering, as if damned—their stomachs swell and they die!

"Our torturers abuse us harshly
While Justice slumbers in a drunken trance!"[21]

He limped a bit further in an unsteady step, sometimes screaming, sometimes speaking more softly:

"The plague, with spade in hand, was wandering
About the land and kept on digging pits . . ."[22]

"He's gone mad!" a woman gasped, frightened.

"He's drunk," said the man walking next to her.

"It's you who have gone crazy," cried Andriy. "It's you who are drunk. This is all written in *The Kobzar*. Have you read it? Do you understand these words? You understand nothing! You are the very people about whom it was written:

"And all the common folk are dumb
And stare with eyes unsure
Like silly lambs: 'Let them!' they say.
'Perhaps it should be thus!'"[23]

Andriy did not notice that he had left the people behind a long time ago, and that they could no longer hear him. He shuffled on and continued talking:

---

[19] *"I mertvym, i zhyvym, i nenarodzhenym,"* ("To the Dead, the Living, and Those Yet Unborn"); Andrusyshyn et al., p. 249.

[20] *"Son,"* ("A Dream"); Andrusyshyn et al., p. 161.

[21] *"Kavkaz,"* ("The Caucasus"); Andrusyshyn et al., p. 243.

[22] *"Chuma,"* ("The Plague"); Andrusyshyn et al., p. 411.

[23] *"Son,"* ("A Dream"); Andrusyshyn et al., p. 161.

"My mother and father and my grandmother and grandfather—they understood. My grandmother had *The Kobzar* memorized—all of it! She always used to say that even the Bible didn't have a greater amount of truth in it. Even when she could hardly move any longer, she'd make her way up to the gate, lean on it, and recite:

> *"For blacker than the grim, black earth*
> *Are those who roam the place in dearth,*
> *The orchards, once so green, have shrunk;*
> *The dwellings have decayed and sunk;*
> *The ponds are overgrown with weeds,*
> *And ruin in the village breeds,—*
> *Its very people witless grow*
> *As dumbly to the field they go*
> *To do forced labor for their lord,*
> *Babies at back, a hungry horde . . ."*[24]

"That's how she talked about the *kolhosp*. The neighbors used to make the 'crazy' sign at her—stirring a finger around one ear—as if to say that her brain was addled from hunger. Not true! My grandmother was of sound mind to the day she died. It is I who have begun to see things clearly only recently. I have come to my senses, and I say to you: '*Come to your senses! Human be, or you will rue it bitterly . . .*[25]

"Come to your senses! Read Shevchenko's *Yurodyvyj* (The Idiot)! Is it not about you? Anyone with the courage to tell you a word of truth is labeled as crazy, a fool. Because you are afraid! I, however, am no longer afraid of anything! If some broad-faced Soviet corporal stood here before me, I would take him on!"

Andriy ranted in this way for a long time, wrenching his soul apart in pain and getting some strange satisfaction out of it. For a long time, he did not pay any attention to the fact that someone was stubbornly pulling on his sleeve, trying to convince him of something. Suddenly he heard the word *"yisty"* (to eat), and he stopped, thunderstruck.

"Huh?" he asked, completely taken by surprise.

---

[24] *"I vyris ya na chuzhyni,"* ("In alien realms my youth was told"); Andrusyshyn et al., p. 387.

[25] *"I mertvym, i zhyvym, i nenarodzhenym...,"* ("To the Dead, the Living, and Those Yet Unborn"), op. cit., p. 251.

A woman stood next to him, and she said, "Enough now! Come with me. I will give you something to eat."

"Eat?" Andriy trembled and took a step back. "No, I don't want to! I am not a beggar. My grandfather, was a Cossack, from the Pivpola clan, did you know that?"

"It shows, lad," replied the woman very seriously. "Come with me!" She took him by the sleeve and led him away with her.

Endnotes
14
Mabut', meni ne vernutys'
Nikoly dodomu . . .

Perhaps I shall not live to see
The home that was so dear to me . . . .

15
. . . . Mynaye,
Neyasnyj den' mij; vzhe smerkaye.
Nad holovoyu vzhe nese
Svoyu neklepanuyu kosu
Kosar nepevnyj . . . Movchky skosyt
A tam—I slid mij zanese
Kholodnyj viter.

. . . My gloomy day then passes by;
Again the sky grows dark;
And the strange mower above my head
Again emerges stark,
Bearing his dull, old scythe along . . .
Soon silently he'll mow me—
Winds will erase my slightest trace,
With nothing left to show me.

16
I dovelos kolys' meni
V chuzhij dalekij storoni
Zaplakat' shcho nemaye rodu

Nema prystanyshcha, Hospody!

But once it was my lot, on distant shores,
To weep because I never had possessed
That refuge sure, a home to call my own . . .

17
Dole de ty? Dole, de ty?
Nema niyakoyi!
Koly dobroyi zhal', Bozhe,
To daj zloyi, zloyi!
Ne daj spaty khodyachomu,
Sertsem zamyraty
I hnyloyu kolodoyu
Po svitu valiatys',
A daj zhyty, sertsem zhyty
I liudej liubyty,
A koly ni . . . . To proklynat'
I svit zapalyty.

Where art thou, Destiny, ah where?
My soul is stirred by none!
If Thou begrudgest me fair fate,
Lord, send a ruthless one!
Let me not sleep when I should wake,
Do not permit my heart to lie
A rotten log that men forsake
And leave in fetid infamy;
But on me let fierce fervor fall
To love all people all my days,
Or let me cast a curse on all
And set the torpid world ablaze!

18
. . . . *Zasnula Vkrayina,*
Burianom ukrylas, tsvilliu zatsvyla,
V kaliuzhi, v boloti sertse prohnoyila
I v duplo kholodne hadiuk napustyla . . . . .

49

Ukraine, alas, has fall'n asleep,
Is overgrown with weeds
And covered deep with slimy mould;
It fails from noble deeds.
Its heart decays in filthy mire
And vipers are allowed
Into its hollows cool to creep . . .

19
Doborolas' Ukraina
Do samoho kraju!

Thus, in her struggle, our Ukraine
Reached the last climax of pure pain!

20
. . . . A onde pid tynom
Opukhla dytyna, holodneye mre.

And there, by the hedge,
A child with swoll'n belly its pangs to allege
Is dying of hunger . . .

21
Katy znushchayutsia nad namy
A Pravda nasha piana spyt'.

Our torturers abuse us harshly
While Justice slumbers in a drunken trance!

22
Chuma z lopatoyu khodyla
Ta hrobovyshcha ryla, ryla.

The plague, with spade in hand, was wandering
About the land and kept on digging pits . . .

23
A bratiya movchyt' sobi
Vytrishchyvshy ochi!
Yak yahniata: "Nekhay,—kazhe—
Mozhe, tak i treba.

And all the common folk are dumb
And stare with eyes unsure
Like silly lambs: "Let them!" they say.
"Perhaps it should be thus!"

24
Chornishe chornoyi zemli
Blukayut' liudy—povsykhaly
Sady zeleni—pohnyly
Bilen'ki khaty, povalialys'
Stavy burianom porosly.
Selo nenache pohorilo,
Nenache liudy podurily,
Nimi na panshchynu idut'
I ditochok svoyikh vedut'."

For blacker than the grim, black earth
Are those who roam the place in dearth,
The orchards, once so green, have shrunk;
The dwellings have decayed and sunk;
The ponds are overgrown with weeds,
And ruin in the village breeds,—
Its very people witless grow
As dumbly to the field they go
To do forced labor for their lord,
Babies at back, a hungry horde . . .

4

Andriy remembered little of what happened after that. Only that he stepped over the threshold of some small house and was given something warm to drink. He then descended into darkness, a darkness full of chaos. In his more lucid moments, Andriy was happily aware of feeling good and of being at peace. He was aware that someone was taking care of him, pulling a blanket over him, adjusting his pillow, offering him something to drink.

After a while, he realized that he was lying on an old sofa in a very small room, and that the drinks he thought of as nothing short of miraculous were simply broth made of barley or dried fruit with a pinch of sugar. He noticed that his caretaker was a tall, older woman who, though dressed in threadbare clothes, had a great dignity about her. She was so dignified, in fact, that Andriy felt a little awkward in her presence, perhaps even a bit frightened. The woman was so thin as to be almost transparent, sparing of words, always composed, and very sad. She did not question Andriy about anything. She did not shower him with either affection or with sympathy. Her restraint made him keep his peace as well.

Still, as soon as Andriy felt strong enough to get up, he asked her, "Do you know the way to Okhtyrka?"

The woman smiled almost imperceptibly, and answered him in a soft, pleasant voice:

"You have asked me that a hundred times! Unfortunately, you were not well enough to give me any further details. Had you been able to give me an address, I would have written to your family and let them know you are alive. We would surely have heard back from them by now."

"By now?" Andriy repeated in surprise. "How long have I been here?"

"Almost two weeks."

Andriy swung his legs down from the sofa, and then lay right back down and said quietly, "There is nobody to write to. I have no one."

He was half-afraid the woman would start questioning him and make a fuss over him, but she did not.

"Well, then there's no reason to be in a hurry," was her only response. "You'll gather up your strength some more and then I will help you on your way."

Andriy was still truly very weak. He tried to get up, but could not manage to support himself on his feet yet.

"What happened to me?" he asked.

"You were weak from hunger and caught a bad cold. Your name is Andriy?"

"Yes!"

He did not have the courage to ask her name, even though he really wanted to. However, it seemed that she was able to read his thoughts.

"My name is Lidia Serhiyivna Cherniavska. Do you know where you are?"

"In Kharkiv, of course!"

"Yes, in Kharkiv, on Bohdanivska Street in a neighborhood known as Osnova. Do you know Kharkiv?"

"No, hardly at all. I've roamed the city for two full days, but I was in a daze."

Andriy was becoming increasingly aware of how much he liked this woman. She was at the same time majestic, simple and direct. Everything about her showed that she was an educated person, and yet she spoke Ukrainian. This was unusual. The majority of educated city dwellers, and even some of the poorest rural folk, preferred to speak Russian—even bad and broken Russian—to speaking their native Ukrainian. They had the notion that this somehow elevated them in other people's eyes. This was a tendency that had taken hold during Tsarist times. This trend had become even more pronounced under the current new regime. Andriy was reminded once more of Shevchenko's words from one of his poems: "I know the language, but don't want to speak it!" But this lady spoke Ukrainian! What a strange and wonderful lady!

Andriy stayed bedridden one day longer, observing with great attention his savior's every move. She was truly different. She did not grumble. She did not complain about how difficult life was. She routinely gave him the lion's share of her own ration of bread and most of the broth that she prepared daily in a small black pot.

Andriy's conscience began to trouble him, and he was feeling ashamed of himself. He felt he did not have the right to accept these things from this feeble, self-sacrificing woman, who was a total stranger to him. So the next day he got up, put on the clothes she had patched and laundered for him, and announced that he was going home.

"Why not stay a little longer?" asked Lidia Serhiyivna. "You said yourself that there was nobody waiting for you in Okhtyrka."

"I'm actually from Hrun', not Okhtyrka," said Andriy quietly. "It's a rather small village in the same region. You've heard of it, perhaps? I had come to Kharkiv to look for work, but nothing came of it. So I'll go back home. At least I will have my own home there."

Lidia Serhiyivna sighed, "It is true that things are always better in one's own home. But will they let you go back?"

Andriy had not thought of the possibility of not being allowed to return to his own home, and this frightened him. True, his family's house was spacious and nice. It was more than likely that some beggar had settled in it by now. Andriy hung his head in thought.

Lidia Serhiyivna proceeded to think aloud: "Of course, the villages have become depopulated, and it would probably be rather easy to find another house. I'm not certain, however, that the authorities will allow an unaccompanied minor to join a *kolhosp*."

"Join a *kolhosp*?" Andriy practically spat the hated word out, anger flaring up in his eyes. "I'd die first before I sign myself up to a *kolhosp*! Even under Tsarist rule, when serfdom held sway in our country, my ancestors were not serfs. Why would I go now and voluntarily place my head in a yoke!"

"If you do not want to enlist in the *kolhosp*," continued Lidia Serhiyivna relentlessly, "and still want to return to the village, you'll end up either in an orphanage or in exile somewhere."

"I ran away from an orphanage once and I will do so again, if they throw me in one! I'll find a way back from exile too!"

Lidia Serhiyivna stood, thinking, placing her hand lightly on Andriy's shoulder as she said in a soft voice, "Wouldn't you like to stay here?"

The suggestion was extremely tempting, but Andriy's pride stood in the way.

"Thank you for these kind words," replied Andriy, choking up with emotion. "The truth is that I'm used to earning my own bread from a very early age, even when I was still living under my father's roof. I don't want to become a parasite now and eat your bread without earning it."

"Don't worry. I'm not one to feed parasites," replied the woman, struggling to hide the smile that was curling up at the corners of her lips.

"Have you some kind of a job for me?" asked Andriy, brightening up a bit.

"Work can always be found. For starters, you can do a few things for me around the house, and then we'll see."

Andriy cast a quick appraising glance around the house and sighed. The home was so old that it gave the feeling of having grown into the ground. There were two tiny rooms, a kitchen, and a hallway. The furnishings were old. Only one solitary tree peeked in from outside the window. How much work could there be here? Clearly, the woman was not being totally honest; she was not letting on that she wanted to keep him because she felt sorry for him. This made Andriy angry.

"Thank you again," he said decisively, picking up his hat. "I will go home."

"May God be with you!" said the woman in a resigned voice. "I'll walk with you for a while. However, should things not go well in the village, be sure to come back. All right?"

Andriy threw her a gloomy look.

"Forgive me. I will only be able to come back if things turn out well and I survive. Otherwise . . . ," his voice trailed off.

The expression on the woman's face turned antagonistic.

"I don't understand you, lad," she said with a hint of coldness and disappointment. "When I met you, I had the impression that you were a boy with spirit and a keen desire to live, and that something could come of you. I see I was mistaken, however."

"I don't know if I have spirit, but I do want to live," said Andriy, somewhat taken aback. "But when I remember the two days I spent wandering the streets of Kharkiv, fear overcomes me. Death is a better alternative!"

"You think it will be different in the village?"

"Hmm! How can I know?" he replied, a bit impatiently. "Listening to you, I wonder. Perhaps it would have been better if I had died that night. It's a pity to have wasted your charity."

The woman's blue-gray eyes softened and clouded over with a shroud of deep sadness.

"Charity, lad, is a nice word," she replied quietly. "But it is not possible to be charitable in times such as these. You see how many people are starving to death out there? How many homeless people are wandering the streets? It is not possible to show mercy to every one of them. I would have walked right past you, as I walk past by hundreds of begging people every day, had you, too, been sitting there mutely with outstretched hands. But you were not. You were arguing, cursing, bellowing out threats. Rebelling. That is what took me by surprise. I thought to myself—too few people in our country are like this young man. We need more people like that. That's why I took you in."

Andriy was suddenly unable to catch his next breath.

"*Pani* (madam) . . . *Titochko* (auntie), how shall I call you to show you my deepest respect? I have to tell you. That's precisely why I want to go back to my village. Those self defense committees . . . I was told about them . . . . Tell me, where should I look for them? I won't betray your confidence. Honest. I promise, I'll go wherever they send me, and I will do whatever they ask me to do, even if I have to die in the process. If you like, I will hold my hand to the fire to prove to you that I am telling the truth!"

The woman gazed at him solemnly and severely, as if accepting his oath, but said nothing. She got up, went to the other room and, bringing in a newspaper, opened it to a certain page and placed it in front of Andriy.

"Read!" she commanded. Andriy noted that she had lost her usual calm demeanor for the first time. He grabbed the paper and read quickly. His body began to shake after the first few lines. The further he read, the more agitated he became. When he had read the entire article, he struck the paper in anger with his fist and ripped it up.

"So! There are Judases out there!" he whispered, remembering the intriguing man at the station. Andriy looked at the woman with unseeing eyes.

"There always were Judases. There are more of them now in these very difficult times."

Andriy was quiet for a long time. He feared he would burst into tears. Then he shook himself out of it and gritted his teeth.

"Well then, perhaps instead of finding my way back to Okhtyrka, it would be better to beat a path to Hvozdyk Krapochka."

"Do you really think that, or is this your despair talking?"

"What else can I do?"

"Endure."

"Endure?!"

"Yes, Andriy, endure!" she repeated firmly. "Endurance is sometimes a test that is more powerful than fire. The government purposely does things to try to turn people into animals, into Judases, into Hvozdyk Krapochkas. They purposely target people like yourself, people who know and can recite Shevchenko by heart. They starve people like that to death, and use other means—extermination, execution, or exile—to bully the others into becoming mute slaves. By joining Hvozdyk Krapochka's band, you will simply be doing exactly what they want. It would be a great shame. People like you ought to live!"

"To live?" echoed Andriy. "To live for what?"

She drew her face closer to his and gave him a steely look.

"One needs to stay alive if only to wait for the right moment to die a meaningful death—an intelligent, useful death." Lidia Serhiyivna spoke quietly and very seriously, carefully enunciating every word. "Do you understand? Life is the greatest gift from God and nobody has the right to squander it for nothing. God gave you an immortal soul, and He has the right to demand it back when it is time. We have to be ready to give it back voluntarily, as one gives back any object that has been borrowed. You may not live to see such a time yourself, but you will teach your children, or even your grandchildren, how, and for what, one must be ready to die. For that, you must live, suffer, and endure, gritting your teeth, and not forget what is happening in villages, in cities, on the roadways of the country now. Do not forget!"

"Forget?" repeated Andriy, with tightly pressed lips. "One does not forget such things!"

He raised his head, looked up at her, and began speaking, as if in confession.

"They came to our home looking for bread, and found half a bag of beets which had been set aside as feed for the livestock. They threw themselves upon my father yelling, 'You, *kurkul* snout! You said you had nothing more! And what's this? WHAT?!' And one of them beat my father over the head with the beets again and again. My mother started crying, 'Don't hit him! You came for grain, for bread, not for beets.' But the man screamed back, 'You were to hand everything over to us—the bread, grain, beets, all of the foodstuff you have!' And again he hit my dad with the beets. My mother grabbed him by the hand and started begging, 'Don't beat him! It was I who hid them. He did not even know.' That inflamed them even more. 'Aaah! *You* hid them! Stealing and concealing from the government! Here, smell this, and be aware what crime this smells of!' He pushed the beets under her nose so hard it began to bleed. Though feeble, my father could not contain himself and threw himself on the man, hitting the official squarely on the jaw with his fist, so hard that the man fell. The other man, a member of *parttysiachnyky*[26] grabbed his revolver and—bang!—into my dad's chest. My father keeled over, and the man said to his entourage, 'Comrades, you are witnesses! This *contra* attacked, and I used my arms in self-defense. To save my life! You hear?!'"

It took everything he had for Andriy not to start crying, and his body trembled convulsively. Two large tears fell from his eyes, rolled down his thin jaws and splattered loudly on the newspaper scattered on the floor.

"They wouldn't even let us bury him, vipers," he said barely audibly. "They took his body and carted it away. They roughed me up also to keep me quiet, for I was ranting and raging. They might have killed me too, but people intervened on my behalf and I ran away. Like a dope, I went to the regional authorities in search of justice. They screamed at me, grabbed me, and placed me in an orphanage. Two months later, two boys from my village were also brought to the same orphanage. They told me that my mother and my two younger brothers died of hunger, and my older sister went away somewhere. I doubt that she was able to get very far . . . ."

Lidia Serhiyivna sat motionless, as if turned to stone, and listened silently. Only her bright eyes narrowed, as she looked far into the distance.

"Well, then, Andriy," she said in an authoritative voice. "Don't go anywhere. Stay here with me."

---

[26]   These were workers, the majority of them illiterate and completely ignorant about agriculture, who were co-opted by the Party to carry out its drive for collectivization. These people were specially trained by the Communist Party for this work. *Parttysiachnyky* were renowned for their brutality and complete lack of compassion. They dressed in civilian clothes and carried pistols, which they liked to use frequently. At first, starting in 1929, 10,000 such were trained, and an additional 5,000 a while later. They got their names—literally meaning "the Party's thousands"—from their numbers.

"How can I stay when I have no documents?" said Andriy, though less belligerently than before. "I cannot get a *propyska*. I cannot get a job. And for me to live like this . . . ."

"Do not worry about this," said Lidia Serhiyivna, interrupting him. "I have friends who will be able to help you get some *dovidky*. Once you have them in hand, you will be able to get a *propyska* and find a job." Bowing deeply, Andriy murmured, "Thank you for this! I will pay you back either after I get a job, or with my labor, or . . . ." Lidia Serhiyivna did not let him finish.

"Of course, of course," she said slowly and with emphasis. "Payment is something that should always be agreed on at the outset. If you were in my shoes, how much would you ask for?"

A hot wave of shame flooded over Andriy, starting from somewhere in the soles of his feet and working its way up to his face. He cast his eyes down, wiped the perspiration off his face, and sobbingly stuttered:

"Forgive me. I would . . . naturally . . . . What you have done for me and propose to do—that's not something one does for money. But I . . . ."

"All right, all right," she said with a slight hint of impatience. "You will be good to have around too. I will help you, and you me, and we will make our way together. At the moment, stay here at home. At about four, start a fire, put some water on to boil, fetch some potatoes from the storeroom and cook them. Here's a chunk of bread for your lunch."

"And you?"

"I'll have some of the fresh loaf. They've promised to deliver a two-day ration today. Now listen, Andriy, you must call me '*baba*' (grandmother). Understand? I will try to make you my grandson from my daughter Tetiana, so you had better start getting used to being my grandson immediately. Have you completed your sixth grade of primary education? Good. This I have to know."

She put on an old fashioned coat and a little black hat as she talked, waved goodbye, and left.

Andriy was left totally bewildered. Somehow he could not imagine himself addressing this proud lady with the simple village name "*baba*." Even the more urbane term, "*babusia*," was not grand enough. But "*baba*?" Lidia Serhiyivna was certainly no "*baba*."

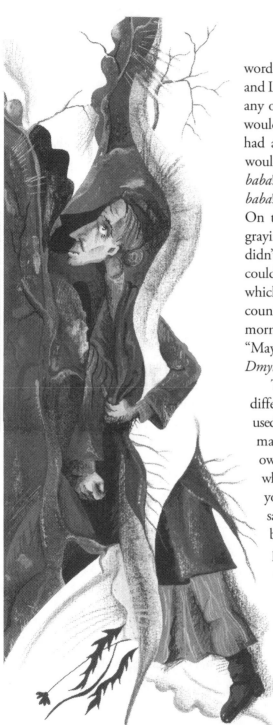

The word "*baba*" is a word with many meanings, and Lidia Serhiyivna did not fit any of them. A young woman would be called a *baba* if she had a bad disposition. People would say: "What a hellish *baba!*" or "What a talkative *baba!*" or "What an ugly *baba!*" On the other hand, calling a graying and aging woman one didn't know very well "*baba*" could be a mark of deep respect which was prevalent in the country's villages, as in—"Good morning, *Baba Ivanykha!*" or "May God help you, *Baba Dmytrykha!*"

The term took on a whole different meaning when it was used in a warm and affectionate manner in reference to one's own grandmother—the one who sang you to sleep, told you stories, put healing salves on your scrapes, stood between you and your parents' anger, kept your secrets, and took the time to make your favorite sweet bread. This *baba* always knew just what to say to soothe. This *baba* was like the sun during springtime—warm and sunny. Nobody in the world could take the place of a child's *baba*. Not even Lidia Serhiyivna, Andriy's savior and benefactor! No, he couldn't call her that! It would be too weird, and too insincere. But then . . . how would he address her? By her name and patronymic? That was how students addressed their teachers at school to show their respect. But this would also sound strange in this case.

Troubled and irritated, Andriy grabbed a broom and went to sweep away the snow. When he got to the gate, he noticed that it was hanging off a hinge, and almost completely torn from the post. He went back to the house, found the appropriate tools and busied himself fixing it.

The sun was shining brightly, but it was a cold day, and the cold pinched his fingers. Andriy rubbed snow into his hands, clapped them together for warmth, and continued working. Just as he finished and stood moving the gate to and fro on the hinge, a little girl of perhaps six ran up to him and stretched out her hand.

"*Diad'ku*, give me something to eat!" she lisped, fixing her bright eyes pleadingly on him.

Andriy was completely taken aback. He couldn't believe that he, a fifteen-year-old, was being addressed as "*diad'ko*" and that someone was asking him—him!—for alms.

He stood there gaping at the young beggar-child. She seemed accustomed to being refused, for a short while later she dropped her hand down and began to walk away.

"Wait, little one!" called Andriy, coming to his senses. "Wait, I'll give you something in a moment."

He ran home and grabbed the chunk of bread Lidia Serhiyivna had left him for lunch. He had never heard of Croesus, but even if he had, this Lydian king with all of his legendary wealth would have seemed, in this moment, an ordinary pauper to him. This piece of bread was a real treasure, not only for her, but for Andriy as well, for Andriy was very hungry and he would have dearly loved to eat the bread himself, yet Andriy was happy to let her have it. This made his gesture a princely deed.

And then something unexpected happened. A little boy ran up to the girl and would have grabbed the bread away from her, had Andriy not intervened. Without even thinking, Andriy stepped up to the boy and pushed him aside with all his might. The little boy fell over sideways, pulling the girl down with him. The children started pummeling each other, fighting over the bread, which was crumbling in the melee. Andriy threw himself between them, trying to separate them, only to be pushed aside by a raggedy woman. She wrested the bread from the hand that held it tightly, divided it in two, and gave each child a half.

"For me! For me!" screamed the boy. "She ate a whole piece yesterday all by herself! This one's for me! All of it!"

"Not yours!" screamed the girl. "I was the one who begged for it and got it! Mother, why did you give him that half? Make him give it back to me!"

"Shush! Or I'll take it away from both of you and eat it myself!" threatened the mother.

Then turning to Andriy, she admonished him, "If you are going to give anything, lad, then give to both. Both of them are equally hungry!" And, almost as an afterthought, she added in a hopelessly sad voice, "It would be best not to give any at all. It would be better for them to die as soon as possible. It's too hard to go on watching their suffering. People are more compassionate towards children. One person gives them something, and then another does as well. But nothing for me!"

She slid down to the ground, sobbing bitterly, and continued, "It doesn't occur to people that a chunk of bread will not save their lives, but only extend their suffering a little while longer and leave them orphans. My days are numbered, and I will die. I won't find peace even in the next world worrying about who will hold them, my poor orphans, to his heart. Who will be at their side when their last hour comes? Who will close their eyes shut? Who will cross their lifeless hands over their chests as they lie dead? Who will sprinkle earth over their dead bodies?"

She cried and sobbed while the children, having gobbled up their portions of bread, were now fighting over the crumbs that had scattered on the ground.

Andriy could not bear to look and listen any more. He hurried back into the house. Inside, he leaned his head on his hands and grew numb. He no longer felt happy. He felt so helpless, so powerless. He had thought he was doing a good deed by giving that child a chunk of bread that he would have gladly eaten himself. But did he? Even if he had a million chunks of bread to hand out to a million starving people, would it make a difference? Yes, one or another of them would live to suffer a day or two longer because of his gift. But he would not be able to help them escape the inevitable. He would only be prolonging their suffering. It was like killing with a dull knife, rather than with a sharp one. What a crazy time, when compassion becomes brutality, and mothers in their great love for their children beg God to take their children away before they themselves die, so that they will not be left alone in the world.

His mind jumped to thoughts about his own family. How had they died? Had his brothers outlived his mother, or had his mother outlived the boys? When did his sister, Yevdokia, leave home? Were the others still alive when she left, or not? Only now did he understand how very important were the answers to these questions. Back then, when his friends told him about the tragedy, this had never occurred to him. Yevdokia was 16, Semen—7, Panko—only 2. His mother probably died first—she would have given all the food to the children. "You are still growing. You need it more," she would have said. She would not have understood that these times called for a very different kind of love from what's usually considered normal. His mother probably had not yet been at wit's end as the mother of these two children was, with her swollen feet swaddled in some rags. For this reason, mother would have sacrificed herself and given everything to her children. In doing so, she would have made a grave mistake, hurting those she loved more than she loved herself. Pan'ko was probably hurt the most. He was such a delightful and darling little boy. Mom hovered over him the most. She would have given him the last bit of available food. Semen would often protest, but mom would say, "Hush, Semen. Pan'ko is so much younger than you! He had never had the milk that you grew up on. Nor cereal boiled in milk. He's small. He probably doesn't even remember milk at all." Yes, that poor child must have paid too high of a price for the care mother lavished on him!

Andriy's imagination began conjuring up terrible images—one more horrible than the next. All of them had to do with his youngest brother, Pan'ko. First he imagined Pan'ko crying under some dry bushes in the fall cold, next Pan'ko moaning alone in a deserted home, and then Pan'ko hugging his mother's cold corpse, calling out "Mommy! Mommy!"

Andriy sat for a long time with his head on the table. Finally, with great effort, he rose to his feet. He had to get busy doing something to drive away these thoughts, which threatened to drive him mad. He threw himself into working on fixing one of the chairs, a very rickety and unsteady one. The work did not come easily, probably because it seemed pointless. But Andriy persisted. He tightened the screws, hammered away, made new holes, put new screws in, and finally finished the job. Finishing one, he started on another, fixing that one as well. Then he began to mend the table leg, and just as he thought of examining the sofa to see if it needed any repairs he heard the gate open. He peered out the window to see a man enter, and he went out to meet him.

The man, a very emaciated farmer, neither old nor young, stood before the small porch with an outstretched hand.

"I have nothing, *dyad'ku*," Andriy tried to say as firmly as possible. "Go with God."

"Perhaps some potato peels, or even some swill water?" begged the man, almost crying.

Andriy's resolve broke.

"Wait." He went back inside, not knowing what he would find. He remembered that Lidia Serhiyivna told him to boil some potatoes. So he went to the cellar, took two potatoes, and brought them out.

"Pardon me for giving you raw potatoes. I don't have cooked ones right now."

"Thank you, thank you!" exclaimed the man, taking the potatoes with trembling fingers. "May God repay you a hundredfold!"

The man turned on his heel and immediately bit into the potato, not bothering to wipe off the dirt. At the gate, he turned to thank Andriy again. But Andriy had hurried back into the house, closing the door behind him. Even inside, Andriy heard the crunching sound of raw potato and dirt as the man chewed.

Ten minutes had not passed when this scene repeated itself. This time it was a young woman, with an infant in her arms, at the door. He couldn't refuse her, and scrambled inside to find something to give her. He found a bag of dried pears. Grabbing a handful, he took them out to her. She looked at him with blank eyes, took the pears and left without even thanking him or saying a word. He didn't know whether it was because she had no more energy, or whether she no longer knew what she was doing. It was precisely for this reason that Andriy felt excruciatingly sorry for her.

"Will she survive long enough to bury her child?" he asked himself, and felt his heart fill with unspeakably heavy pain.

He didn't have time to think much further about the woman, for another came to the door. She was a young girl, approximately his age.

"For the love of God, please give something!"

He couldn't refuse her either. He went down to the cellar again, brought up two carrots and handed them to the girl. But as soon as she left, he closed the gate after her and locked it.

"I'm giving away food that is not mine without even asking permission," he scolded himself. "In addition to eating her food myself, I am giving to others the food she denies herself!"

He had no right to give away the food. Had Lidia Serhiyivna acted in such a way, she would have had to go begging a long time ago. At that moment he also knew that he could not but give. Whether it was his own food or someone else's, the moment his eyes fell on a look so full of suffering, so imploring, so full of humiliation—he would give it all away. Yesterday and the day before that he was in a better position. Nobody asked him for anything, so his conscience did not bother him.

He caught a glimpse of a silver pocket watch hanging over Lidia Serhiyivna's bed, as he went to start a fire. Once again someone was knocking on the door. Andriy decided not to go out. But the knocking persisted with insistence, as if making it perfectly clear that the person at the door had no intention of leaving. This could have been Lidia Serhiyivna herself finally coming back home, so Andriy went and opened the door. No, it was not the lady of the house, but a boy. He, too, was there to beg for food.

Angry, not so much at the guest as at himself, Andriy began to scream loudly, "There is nothing! Get away from here and don't knock anymore!"

"And why are you screaming, why are you so mad, you jerk?" replied the lad in a dignified, but cold, manner. "If you haven't got the heart to part with a few leftovers, then choke on them!"

"Leftovers?" shouted Andriy, boiling over in anger. "I gave away the last crumb early this morning and am sitting here hungry myself, while for the last hour or so, you have all been coming one after another, like locusts! What can I possibly give all of you to eat?!"

The boy glanced at Andriy, simultaneously sniffing his nose and straightening his worn-out sheepskin hat, and without a trace of malice replied:

"I guess all of them must have been people who had been waiting in line hoping to get bread. We've all been standing there since nightfall, and they only delivered the bread at about noon. They say there were five hundred loaves, but there were three thousand people in line. The first few in line got some. The rest—nothing! So we thought we'd wait until the next delivery tomorrow. But the damned militia came and dispersed us all. Unable to purchase bread, the people scattered all about begging for a piece of bread. And once again, it's just like being in line—whoever gets there first might get something, the rest get thrown out to the dogs, just as you are doing to me right this minute."

The boy was only about twelve years old, and somehow he did not look like one of those starving people dulled by hunger. He was, however, so thin, that he looked more like a toy figure fashioned out of straw. But he had a sense of humor, and a gleam in his intelligent eyes.

"Hey, bro," he said out of the blue. "Aren't you one of us too?"

"What do you mean 'one of us?'" asked Andriy disconcertedly.

"Don't try to weasel out!" the boy shot back. "Not only your clothes, but your snout betrays that you are from a village. Have you family here?"

"Yes, I have a grandmother," lied Andriy unconvincingly.

"Your grandmother lives here? Oh, how lucky you are that she has taken you in. My situation is exactly the opposite. My grandmother did not take me in, rather I took her out of the village. And now I have to take care of her everywhere we go. It's hard."

"How did you manage to take her, and what for?" asked Andriy, not understanding.

"How can one talk with an idiot like you!" scowled the boy contemptuously. "What for? What could I do with her? You know how it is in the village. Of our whole family, my grandmother and I are the only ones who have survived. I decided to leave the village, so I had to take her with me."

"And what have you been doing?"

"Nothing. Some drunkard has taken us in. He, too, lives only on what he can beg from others, though he says he has some kind of a pension and ration cards. So that's how we live. Grandmother stays home because she cannot walk, and I go out and try to find a way to get something for us. I beg some, and steal some. That's how we get by. See, I've even got enough to buy a kilo loaf of commercial bread. If only I had gotten to that queue earlier last night! But, as you see, I didn't have good luck."

"So you don't have a *propyska*?"

"No. We have no identification papers, so we cannot get a *propyska*. We were being shoved from one place to another like homeless dogs until this drunkard let us stay with him. He's not afraid of anyone—neither the militia nor Stalin himself, probably because he's always drunk and doesn't give a damn. He let us have his bed, his kerosene stove, and even his down comforter. He says he doesn't need anything other than his whiskey. He says that a drunkard always falls off a bed anyway, and might set the house on fire. I'm telling you, he's a complete basket case."

The boy pushed up his worn-out cap, sniffled and cursed:

"May they all eat dirt, and their mothers too! Imagine, standing in line all night long and having to go back home with nothing! And grandmother is waiting hungry. Had I known earlier that I would not be able to get the bread, I would have gone to the bazaar to buy a cup of millet at least. But I thought that a kilo of bread was the better deal than a bowel of porridge, so I kept standing in that line. I myself am not hungry. I was lucky enough to get a whole bowl of cooked lentils from a young schoolteacher—and very grateful to her I am for that!" the boy continued, patting himself happily on his flattened stomach, none the plumper from the lentils he had just eaten. "I'd be happy just to crawl under a blanket and go to sleep. But I feel sorry for my grandmother."

Andriy liked this young boy and felt bad for his hungry grandmother.

"You say you have something to cook on?"

"Yes, something to cook on and something to cook in, but nothing to cook."

Andriy went into the house once again, took out the tin with barley, poured out two handfuls into some newspaper, folded it up and brought it to the boy.

"Ah, so you see," said the boy, winking. "It's no wonder I've been talking up a storm here with you. I saw immediately that you are a clever boy. And I've managed to talk my way to getting some dinner for my grandmother. To your health! If ever the fields back home become fertile again, I will pay you back with interest! In the meantime, write. Don't forget about us!"

Winking again, he hurried down the street, happy as a lark. Andriy watched him take leave with delight. What a little devil! A person like that will always land on his feet, no matter what! Not only is he managing well for himself, he's also supporting his grandmother.

Back inside, Andriy put on the pot of potatoes to cook. A gloomy mood—a mixture of anger, depression, and guilt—descended upon him.

What a soft head and heart he had. He had given away two potatoes, two carrots, a handful of dried pears and two handfuls of barley. At one time this would have seemed like nothing at all. Now, however, the value of every crumb and every morsel of food had radically changed. Fear at having given away so much enveloped him. The worst part was that he had given away food that was not his in the first place. No! He had no right to do that! He must not dare give any more away.

He held on to this decision—twice. Each time, a woman had stood at the door, begging. Twice he refused firmly, decisively, in anger even. Everything inside him cramped up in sorrow and shame, and he was so fiercely angry that it was all he could do to stop himself from cursing. He was angry first and foremost with himself for not having the right to give alms, for he himself had nothing. He was angry, secondly, at them—the people at the door, because they did not know the truth of the situation and, therefore, did not understand. He was even angry at the black pot that was boiling over on the stove, filling the house with the pungent smell of boiled potato peels. It would be better if there were no pot, no potatoes, no dried pears, no barley, nor any carrots! Then his conscience would not bother him and he would not have to be so distressed. Then he would not have to make that oppressively difficult decision—to give or not to give.

A new knock on the door made him go weak at the knees. He didn't even want to get up from his chair. But the knocking persisted—again and again. He struggled to get hold of himself, as he got up and went to the door. On his way to the door, Andriy tried despairingly to think of how he would say "no." Would he do so with an apology, or by making excuses, or by feigning heartlessness, or simply by turning the person away?

When he opened the gate with a sharp tug, an indescribable joy came over him to suddenly see that it was Lidia Serhiyivna standing there. The possibility that it might be her had not crossed his mind this time. Suddenly, the word he had so much trouble with that morning and that had seemed so presumptuous on his part to say, just burst out of him naturally and with complete sincerity:

"*Baba*! It's you! I thought it was going to be yet another starving person!"

Freed of feeling the burden of responsibility for yet another alms-seeker, Andriy was so happy that he would have been ready to kiss

Lidia Serhiyivna'a hands and feet. He led her into the house with great care and respect, helped take off her cloak and soggy shoes, brought her old slippers and helped put them on, sat her down on a stool and threw a warm shawl over her shoulders. He saw that she was numb from the cold and exhausted, and so he made her rest and did not allow her to lift a finger.

"You just tell me what needs to be done and I'll do it," he said.

Lidia Serhiyivna had brought home a partially eaten ration of bread, six pieces of chocolate, two onions, and two herring with their head and tail ripped off. The two of them ate the potatoes with the herring and onions, drank some hot water with chicory "coffee" and had the chocolate for dessert.

Afterwards Andriy gathered up his courage to ask, "*Baba*, will you go out again tomorrow?"

"Yes, Andriy, I will. I'll have to go out this evening to get a place in line for the commercial bread. From there, I will be going to some government offices to try to settle things for you. This will probably take all day."

"I will go and stand in line this evening. You are too tired. But, tomorrow, when you go out, please lock the gate."

"I can't. The gate is broken. It has settled too far into the ground. You'll just have to close it with the latch, just as you did today."

"I've fixed the gate. You can use the key now"

"You've fixed it? Wonderful! It always worried me to leave the house without being able to lock it. I did have a second key somewhere at one time. I'll look for it and give it to you so that we can be independent of each other."

"I don't need a key!" cried Andriy, raising his arm up as if to shield himself from something. "Shut me in so that I will not be able to go out."

"So you won't be able to get out? What's gotten into your head???"

Andriy stood dumbfounded.

"It's b-b-be-c-cause those s-s-tarving p-p-people c-c-come kn-n-ocking, kn-n-ocking . . ." he stammered. "And I c-c-can't . . . ."

Hanging his head down guiltily, Andriy confessed how much he had given away that day and to whom. He expected to be reproached, and was quite ready to accept her words in silence. But what he heard was something completely different.

"Andriy, you can give or not give, but to hide and have someone lock you in—that's just shameful. Truth must always be faced squarely. But you propose to stick your head in the sand instead, like an ostrich."

She kept looking at him with a stern gaze, knitting her brows austerely. Andriy withered under that gaze and under the coldness of her voice. He felt miserable.

"But *Baba*!" he cried out. "If you don't lock me in, I will give away every bit of food you have in the house to the last crumb!"

"Then give it away!"

"But what right do I have to give it away when it's not mine?"

"Then don't give it away!"

"But the problem is I can't do that either! I turned away two women with nothing, and still feel the pain of this in my heart. How can I not give them something when they might not have had anything to eat for days?"

"Then you should have given them something."

It felt like she was making a fool of him, but no, Lidia Serhiyivna was totally serious, and this confused him even further.

"If it were mine, I'd give it away!" he practically screamed in deep despair. "I would give everything away, and that would be that!"

She looked at him with the same dispassionate gaze, and said calmly, "Well then, Andriy, I give you everything that is in this house, and you have my permission to do whatever you want with it. Give it away!"

"And afterwards—how will we survive?" he said, wringing his hands. "Walk around, too, with outstretched palms? Or die of hunger?"

"Well, this is the decision you will have to make for yourself—either one or the other. But I will not lock you in. It is shameful, son, to hide from reality!"

He thought and thought, and then sighed hopelessly, "Oh, it's all for naught! Even if one were to give everything away, one would still not be able to avert the disaster."

"That's true. They say that there are 20 million people starving in Ukraine today. The rest of the population, with a few exceptions, is half-starving. The cities, after all, are also kept on semi-starvation rations, so there isn't much food available to help the starving. Consequently, if each half-starved city dweller shared his food with one starving person, both of them would eventually die of hunger. It's simple mathematics."

"The conclusion, then, seems to be not to give anyone anything. Let those 20 million croak. Is that it?" asked Andriy, giving his benefactress a hostile look and suddenly losing the warm feelings he had for her.

Lidia Serhiyivna looked at him reproachfully.

"First of all, Andriy, people do not *croak*—people *die*. Secondly, it is unlikely that all of those 20 million starving will actually die. People say that about three million have already perished, and that another five million will follow suit.

Her voice suddenly broke and her eyes misted over.

"You see, Andriy, how they've rounded these numbers," she said detachedly. "Three million, five million . . . A few hundred thousand more, a few hundred thousand less . . . What's the difference? Human existence is now being rounded up to the nearest million."

She recovered herself quickly, and continued.

"And thirdly, son, the human soul has something of the divine in it, which is why it prevails over cold reason. One cannot help everyone, but at least one can give a little something to someone, even if it means ripping it out of one's own mouth. Today, I took pity on a dog. He was sitting next to a young boy, and he was in such bad shape, so thin, so shabby-looking, and had a look of great suffering in his eyes. At least a person can talk, beg, complain. But an animal is mute! That little dog was sitting next to his young master, as he will continue sitting next to that lad's dead body, until they kill him off too."

Only now did Andriy understand why the herring they had for dinner were missing heads and tails, and why the loaf of bread had a piece missing.

"And the little boy? Was he still alive?"

"Barely. He was no longer even able to eat. Whatever food I gave him, the dog ate."

Andriy was ashamed at how he had spoken to this kind woman and of the tone of voice he had used.

5

True to her word, Mrs. Cherniavska gave Andriy a lot of work to do around the house. He was glad of it, for he was industrious by nature. His routine was fairly simple. At night, he would go out and bring water back from the public tap. Then he would dress warmly, bundle up his feet and ankles with extra strips of padded cloth, grab an old pillow, and go out to stand in a queue in front of the nearest "*lariok*" (a small wooden hut which sold bread, beer, herring, and the like). Once there, Andriy would alternate between standing and sitting on the pillow when he got tired. Sometimes, he even allowed himself to doze off a bit. He couldn't do this often or for very long, for quarrels and even fights had a way of erupting frequently, and it was all too easy to lose one's place in line in the ensuing melee. Also, the militia would sometimes come and disperse the crowd. They always threatened to arrest anyone who ventured back before six o'clock to encourage people to stay away. Most people knew better than to believe these threats, so they would make a great show of leaving and then hide around one corner or another just a few blocks away, only to hurry right back after the militia left to assume a place in line again.

Some of the fiercest battles between people happened right after such disruptions, for those who had been at the head of the line always wanted to resume their "rightful" place. However, those who were quicker at getting back argued that this was not a visit to the theater, with tickets and reserved seating, and insisted that a place in line was strictly on a first come, first served basis.

And so, every night from Monday to Friday, Andriy would stand in line until four or five o'clock in the morning. Then Lidia Serhiyivna would come to take his place, while he ran home, ate some soup, and fell in total exhaustion on the couch to sleep. After the long sleepless night in the freezing cold, he usually wouldn't get up until noon. By that time, the mistress of the house had come back and gone out again. If their efforts had been successful that day, a kilogram of commercial bread would be on the table. On average, they managed to procure a loaf two out of the five times they stood in line. The other three times they had to make do with whatever supplies they had in the house and with what food they could manage to get on Lidia Serhiyivna's ration cards.

Once up, Andriy would eat some bread, drink some "coffee," and tidy up the house. Since they never managed to find the second key to the house, Lidia Serhiyivna, against her better judgment, did lock Andriy in the house when she left for the day. However, this did not bring Andriy the peace of mind he had hoped for. He continued to live in a state of constant tension, always anticipating a knock on the door. When it came, he gritted his teeth and clenched his fists, and was overcome with feelings of shame. He hated himself for hiding in the face of human suffering in such a cowardly manner. He felt it would be better to go out and state boldly and outright that he would give nothing, rather than to hide inside, like a rat in its hole.

The gate itself was like a fine-tuned musical instrument, conveying with great clarity the emotional state of the person knocking. At times, the knocks sounded fearful and quiet. At others, they let out a despairing sob. There were the times of insistent rapping, or the shaking of mad despair. Andriy did not have to go out and look to get a clear picture of what was going on in the street. Though separated by a closed gate and looking out through a double-paned window, he saw, heard and understood everything. What should he do? Dear God, what was one to do?

Suddenly, Andriy came up with an idea. Instead of giving small amounts of bread to every person who knocked, from now on every time there was a knock on the door he would set aside in a bag the portion he would have given. When the bag was full, he would give it to one person. That way, he hoped to be able to fully satisfy the hunger of at least one person. He put this idea into action immediately. The minute he heard a knock, he placed a small piece of bread into the bag. This helped to assuage his conscience.

The relief he felt at arriving at this solution did not last long. That evening, Lidia Serhiyivna saw the bag and asked about it.

A bit embarrassed, Andriy explained.

"It's for the starving," he began. "I just cannot clear out of my mind the image of the young woman with her children, or of my own mother and my younger brothers . . . . By continuing to give just a morsel of bread to many people, I will not save anybody. So I thought of setting aside a piece of bread every time there's a knock on the door and then, when the bag is full, giving the whole bagful of bread away to one fortunate person. In that way, at least one hungry person will be fully sated."

Lidia Serhiyivna looked at him with sympathy, and silently put the bag back where she had found it.

"You're not angry with me, *Baba*, are you?"

"Why would I be? Your intentions are good; however, the devil that's behind the Kremlin's star will only have some fun with them. For the devil makes sport of everything and can take even the best idea and cast doubt on it."

"Let him. I don't care."

"You don't care because you're thinking is a bit superficial, son. You are preparing to feed one hungry person. But the devil will come along and ask, 'Why only one? Where's the fairness in that?'"

"By that logic, did you act unfairly by taking me in off the street?"

"That's precisely the problem, Andriy. In these times it is hard to determine what is fair and what isn't. You have been with me now for almost three weeks. I could have let almost 20 people benefit from a day's worth of warmth and food, one by one, in that period of time. So, the question is—am I acting fairly or unfairly?"

Andriy immediately pricked up his ears.

"I don't understand you, *Baba*," he said, offended. "Do you regret letting me stay here? If so, no problem, I'll be on my way."

"Your going away will again only delight the devil, for he will say, 'You might have saved at least that one person. By letting a new person into the house each day to enjoy a day's worth of warmth, you will have saved nobody.'"

"It's terrible to listen to you, *Baba*!" complained Andriy. "It seems that one way is bad, and the other way is not good. So what should we do? Should we do nothing? Should we stand idly by and watch people die of hunger?"

"Andriy, you are seeing only the people who are dying of hunger—the farmers. You pity them. You even understand that their death, taken not individually, but as the group as a whole, is tantamount to the death of independent agriculture in our country. However, a nation is made up of more than just farmers. There are the industrialists, the traders, the politicians, the military, the clergy, the scientists and academics, and the artist. All of them are an important piece of the foundation that supports a nation's unique identity and its independence. You do not see these people in the ranks of farmers dying out. These people have already been either killed, imprisoned, or exiled . . . .

"Tragic as that is, the fate of those who have not been imprisoned, but have been allowed to live free, is far worse. For they will continue working, only now they will be working for the destroyers of the nation's statehood, for those who endeavor to destroy the people and the independence of the nation. The death of millions is always a tragedy, but it could be transformed into a triumph, if it were to serve the good of the nation and bring glory to the nation. We have the example of this in the Spartans back in the times of the Greeks. You probably have never heard of the Spartans, and will have to read up on them. To cite another example, in the time of Nero, thousands of Christians died in coliseums, on crosses, or burned at the stake, and their sacrifice, their steadfastness, and their blood gave rise to a faith so strong that they forced the very foundations of hell to tremble. But today, millions are dying and Satan is laughing hysterically, because he is reinforcing his fortress with their bones. For this reason, Andriy, a bagful of bread, or even a thousand or a hundred thousand such bagfuls, will not help find a way out of this evil if giving it will help to salve our consciences and put them to sleep. What we need is people again willing to sacrifice their lives, on a scale more numerous than the victims of the famine. We must prepare our spirits and our hearts for them."

Andriy listened attentively, trying to commit every word to memory. Something strange was happening in his soul. Nobody had ever talked to him like this before. He intoned a voiceless "amen" at Lidia Serhiyivna's last words.

> *"And in our land, by faith retrieved,*
> *No foemen shall be brought to birth,*
> *Mothers and sons shall show their worth*
> *And love shall reign throughout the earth."*[27]

Andriy was under the influence of this conversation for a number of days. He behaved in his usual way and followed his normal routine—fixing

---

[27] Taras Shevchenko, *"I Arkhemid I Halilay,"* ("Old Archimedes drank no wine"): Andrusyshyn et al., p. 546. See endnote for this chapter for transliterated Ukrainian version.

things in the house, bringing in water from the tap, taking his place in the bread line, eating, sleeping. He continued setting aside a morsel of bread at every knock. All the time, however, he was mulling over the new information Lidia Serhiyivna had given him, information he had never known before. Nonetheless, shortly before Lidia Serhiyivna was due to return home, Andriy's mind turned to wondering whether she had managed to make any progress with regard to his status. When she did come home, however, and said nothing on the topic, he realized that it was pointless to ask, for if there had been any news, whether good or bad, she would have told him herself. Clearly, her silence meant there wasn't any news to report.

Then came the weekend. Both of them were at home, and Andriy began asking for all sorts of explanations: about the Spartans, about the people who had been killed or destroyed in other ways, those who were not among "the starving." Lidia Serhiyivna answered his questions with great care, and Andriy began to learn things he had never known before. He learned about those who were executed for taking part in actions aimed at gaining Ukraine's independence, about the destruction of the Ukrainian Autocephalous Orthodox Church, about the campaign against leading Ukrainian academics and cultural figures, as well as about the people who were forced to "change their colors" in order to save their own lives and that of their families.

Listening, Andriy was overcome with sadness, anger and indignation. So this is how it was? Moscow was not satisfied merely with robbing the peasants' of their bread and their property, but took that which was dearest to them from each and every person? They took away liberty! They took away the freedom to live, to move about, to create and to think freely! The famine was not an end in itself, but a way to make people worry solely about mere survival, about where to get that next piece of bread, and therefore to have no time to devote to matters of a higher order. Truly, only Satan could have dreamt up something like this!

At night, as he took his place in the queue again, Andriy became convinced that *baba* was right and that she was telling the truth. The people around him—what were all of them talking about? Listening to them, it seemed like they were talking about many things, but really all their thoughts were centered on food. All their quarrels were about bread and about food. Food was perennially on everybody's mind. Getting food was everyone's ultimate aim and the object of all their striving. People stooped to all sorts of levels to get food. For food, they begged, borrowed, stole, surrendered their dignity, and were willing to hurt one another without mercy or compassion.

Lidia Serhiyivna came to take his place in line at five in the morning. He returned home more tired than ever. He ate breakfast, lay down, and could not fall asleep for a long time because these thoughts would not give him any peace.

He woke up late and walked into Lidia Serhiyivna's room to look at the watch, as was his habit. The watch had disappeared. This unsettled Andriy, and he did not know what to think. He couldn't believe that Lidia Serhiyivna had taken the precaution to put the watch away in a safe place. Could she have sold it or bartered it for something? The thought depressed, even angered, him. After all, they did not need anything; they were not dying of hunger! A whole loaf of bread lay on the table—the prize for a night spent in the queue. It was enough for them to get by on. The watch had belonged to *baba's* deceased husband, and it meant a lot to her. Perhaps it has stopped, and she had taken it in for repairs?

It was an overcast day, with no sun. It wasn't so easy to determine what time it was without a watch on a day like today. Andriy could not quite make up his mind whether it was getting close to dinner and he should start preparing it, or whether it was still much earlier in the afternoon.

At a loss, Andriy sat down opposite Lidia Serhiyivna's bedroom. The door to the bedroom stood ajar, and he took a closer look at the furniture in the house as he sat, actually really taking note of it for the very first time. An old nickel-plated bed stood in the bedroom, together with an armoire, a commode, a bookcase full of books, and a small bed stand with mother-of-pearl and bronze carvings. The furniture was all fashioned of light-colored wood, and it was very old and beautifully carved in whimsical designs. It looked very expensive. Even the old couch Andriy slept on and the round dining table and chairs with high backs and the faded design pressed into the leather, spoke of a bygone era of material comfort. This furniture could not have been bought for this house. Certainly not!

The bedroom window looked out onto a small garden full of soot-covered snow. A thin young pear tree stood in the center. It was the fruit of that tree, dried, that has been supplementing their meager diet. Andriy looked at the tree and shook his head. It was clear that whoever planted it did not have the mind of a gardener, for the tree was planted smack in the center of the garden. Come summer, it would throw its shade over the entire garden. So they would not be able to plant potatoes and vegetables there. The tree should have been planted over to one side.

Andriy's feeling for the earth and for agriculture began to come alive again. He began thinking of what he could plant in Lidia Serhiyivna's garden in the spring. His reverie was broken when she herself entered the room, a basket overflowing with goods in her hands, and a look of great satisfaction on her face.

"Well Andriy, I greet you with good news," she said.

She took out two pieces of paper from her bag, each folded into quarters, and handed them to him. Andriy took them, unfolded one and read it, then the other. They took his breath away. He kept shifting his glance from the papers to her and back again, and he could not believe his eyes!

"*Baba*," he managed to say through a tight throat. "These documents are real!"

She smiled. "Real or not, with them in hand, you will be able to carve out a life."

"But the name is mine!" he began reading it off the document: "*Andriy Yakymovych Pivpola.* Exactly!"

"Of course it's yours," she continued smiling. "Even if someone should recognize you here, there will be no trouble. You'll simply say that you had been put into an orphanage and then left. And that is all."

"Does this mean that I can get a *propyska* here in Kharkiv?"

"Yes, we will go tomorrow and do just that. And then we will go and sign you up in school."

"Yes, I see—to the Factory Trade Institute. Do they teach all kinds of trades there?"

"Yes. You will learn a trade, get a free lunch every day, and even receive a small stipend in addition. You will also have your own ration cards."

This was unbelievable! It was like a dream. Andriy was in a daze. He kept reading and rereading the documents, scrutinizing the official stamps, and nervously pushing back his hair—slightly too longish now—from his face. Lidia Serhiyivna, in the meantime, was unpacking her basket—two warm winter shirts, a pair of pants, a warm wool sweater, a quilted coat, two pairs of undergarments, a hat with ear flaps and even a pair of gloves.

"I think these will fit you, even though they are second-hand. Now, all you need is shoes. We'll buy them tomorrow."

She cast a glance at the dumbfounded boy, and quipped, "Come now, Andriy, how about a 'thank you?'"

He looked at her with unseeing eyes, still in a daze.

"Thank you?" he repeated quietly. "How can I possibly thank you, *Baba*?"

"Perhaps the way they taught you at home?"

He took a step forward, carefully took her hand into his, bent over it and kissed it gently and with reverence. This gesture—and the care with which Andriy did it—was more eloquent than even the most flowery words and the most enthusiastic gestures. Lidia Serhiyivna was moved.

"May God be with you, son," she said soothingly. "I am very pleased that things worked out so well."

But reality knocked on the gate, at once putting an end to their conversation and their excitement. Without even asking permission, Andriy took the loaf of bread that was on the table, cut it in half, and added it to the morsels he had collected in the bag. Taking the key from *baba*, he went outside. He did not bother to see whether the beggar was a man or a woman. He saw only a trembling emaciated outstretched hand that grabbed the bag greedily. Andriy stood outside in the cold for a while, and then went back in. He picked up the documents, read through them again, and placed them on the table.

"Y-e-s-s!" he sighed, feeling something like a mixture of guilt and shame. "You, *Baba*, have been able to save one person, but you will not be able to save another. You don't have another silver watch."

His words did not seem terribly important, but they caused Lidia Serhiyivna to jump with a start, and the expression on her face changed. She looked like she might reproach him, or start crying. In a flash, she took hold of herself and, avoiding his eyes, said quietly:

"Andriy. You must never ever mention this again. You hear? Never!" Then she commanded, in a severe tone, "Light the stove!"

She left, walked into her bedroom and shut the door behind her. Andriy was left—mouth half-open, and with a bitter feeling of having unwittingly committed a grievous error.

Endnotes
27
I na onovlenij zemli
Vraha ne bude, supostata,
A bude syn, I bude maty,
I budut' Liudy na zemli.

And in our land, by faith retrieved,
No foemen shall be brought to birth,
Mothers and sons shall show their worth
And love shall reign throughout the earth.

6

Andriy enrolled in the metal-working department of the school. Here, his skill with his hands and attentiveness to the work quickly earned him the good will of his teachers. Though the subject was new to him, the work ethic he learned at home as a child and his own industrious spirit served him well. The first project the students were required to do was to file a piece of metal into a perfect square. It took him only four days to complete the work, while it took other students two months and even, in some cases, three months to do so.

Professor Khomenko, a strict and demanding craftsman, looked over Andriy's work with evident satisfaction.

"You've studied somewhere before?"

"Umm . . . yes, I studied lots of things," said Andriy evasively.

Khomenko gave him a quizzical look but asked no further questions, saying only, "Tomorrow you will report for work."

Andriy was surprised that he was being sent to work at the Kharkiv Steam Engine Construction Factory, and not in the school workshop, as he had assumed. This factory, like most others at this time, was operating on a special—"let's close the gap"—work regimen, for it had fallen far behind the overly optimistic production quotas set by the state. Older students from all the trade schools in the area were brought in to help, as there was also a shortage of qualified labor, despite the thousands of unemployed people wandering the streets of the city. True, these unemployed people were not specialists in the construction of steam engines, but they were certainly capable adults and could have easily taken the place of the students who, apart from still being minors, were also not very skilled—and certainly less motivated—to work. The hard regimen at the factories quickly exhausted the most hard-working among them. Many were so tired after their shift that they either skipped school or stopped showing up for work. There was no way to force them to work at the factory. Child labor was against the law. Those students who continued to show up tried to get away with

81

as little work as possible. They loafed around, played hide and seek, and got into all sorts of mischief. Few were like Andriy, who continued to work diligently and conscientiously. Even many of the adult employees at the factory worked only at half steam—slowly and half-heartedly. Wherever possible, they simply went through the motions. Most of their time was spent in complaining about the low wages, the long hours, and the insufficient amount of food they were able to buy with their ration cards.

The only people who worked really hard were the master craftsmen. They were directly responsible to management for the fulfillment of the norms. They tried to mobilize their subordinates to keep up a steady pace of work in every way possible—with appeals to their dignity and to their sense of honor, and with threats of reprisal, as well. They devised such original phrases for shaming people into action, that even a poet might have been envious of their skill and been tempted to borrow one or two of their turns of phrase. It was almost impossible to refrain from cursing at times, for there were shortages of the most essential materials and parts, and even of an adequate supply of electricity, which was available only in spurts. This disrupted and slowed down the work at every step, as did the antiquated machinery at the factory, which frequently broke down, causing further disruptions. It was not easy to set a consistent pace of work and to stick to it under such circumstances.

Management did not want to know anything about this disastrous state of affairs at the factory. They tried to convince everyone that the problems could be overcome by intensifying political education among the workers. The gist of this education, which was repeated over and over again, went something like this: "Yes, if we all pull together, we can fulfill—and even over-fulfill—the quotas." Many master craftsmen truly did their best to advance the cause and "reeducate" the workers. But their efforts were often at the expense of the workers' health, and sometimes even at the expense of their lives.

Andriy tried to keep as low a profile at work as possible. He had learned his lesson well about being enthusiastic about work from the young man he had met when he first came to Kharkiv—the one who had cursed him out for his enthusiasm, but later ended up saving him from the Party boss at the work site. The truth of the matter was, however, that it wasn't in his nature to loaf around. Whatever the task at hand, he did it quickly and well. Obviously, he was not given work that required the refined skills of a professional. But even without such skills, he found many ways to be useful. If asked to secure a spinney, he would do so in a way that really held. When asked to clean a rusty piece of machinery, he did so until it shined. When asked to run an errand to another department, he obeyed quickly and without any detours. When asked to lend a hand, he did so with patience and a steady hand. Moreover, he paid close attention to the professionals at work, and was always ready to lend them a hand—to pass a needed tool, to help lift or support something, to anticipate problems or warn of some impending danger. In so doing, he called attention to himself, albeit unintentionally. People at the factory—the foremen and master craftsmen as well as the other workers—all liked him.

"That tyke over there," said one of the foremen, "you can tell immediately that he comes from the working class. Whose kid are you?" he asked, turning to Andriy.

Without much thought, Andriy shot back crisply, "The son of the Commissioner of the Committee of Heavy Industry, sir!" His quick retort was met with a round of hearty laughter.

"Oh yes, of course! Naturally! Everything about you makes it clear you are telling the truth!" And they all liked him all the more. As a result, Andriy was pulled in all directions at work, for every master craftsman wanted him to be a member of his brigade. Craftsmen and professional workers alike treated Andriy seriously, speaking with him as if he were an equal in age and experience.

Andriy was able to forget about everything at work. But reality accosted him again as soon as he stepped out of the door of the factory and kept him company all the way to his next destination. The number of starving was growing with every passing day, and their corpses littered the streets of the city ever more densely. Life in Ukraine's capital, however, kept moving right along at a fast pace, as if completely unaware of what was happening all around. Trams and buses hummed by, filled to overflowing, and people hurried about their business. Cinemas were showing films, and theaters were showing plays—comedies and tragedies—and staging opera productions. At the same time, another drama was playing itself out under every billboard, under every posted program and cinema schedule. It was a human drama which required no advertising, no make-up, no props and no tickets.

This drama far exceeded in scope the tragic imagination of even the gloomiest of dramatists. Each element of this drama would have broken to bits the hearts of the hardest and meanest of people had it been written up, staged, and performed in front of a live audience. The fact that it was multiplied by millions and became such a mass and common everyday phenomenon encountered on the streets meant that people grew indifferent. Few of even the more sensitive people, who were not able to pass by without placing a little something into the outstretched skeletal hand of one or another person, had the insight to comprehend the full scope of the tragedy. For what they were seeing was only the final act of a drama whose first acts had been played out beyond the borders of the city in the rural areas of the country. Only the people who had been tied to their land for generations and who had a deep and abiding love for that land, could grasp the full measure of this tragedy. These were the people who had a deep bond with the land, with their bit of earth, a bond that was as strong as an infant's bond with its mother. Being forced to break that bond was tantamount to giving up one's life.

Only now, when he had a roof over his head and a job to go to, did Andriy begin to feel an overpowering longing for his native village, for the home where he had been born, for the orphaned land that would wait vainly for the loving touch of the calloused hands of its owners. For Andriy, as for each farmer, the earth was alive; the earth was like a kin—it was something very dear. These people knew that this land was holy! No, he was not thinking of the land here in the city that had been paved over or set in cobblestones, that had tram lines running over it and electrical wires strung above it from posts that had been hammered into it along the length of the streets. No, the land he and the peasants loved so much was the earth that crumbled under the plow, the earth that smelled of dew and greenery, the earth that stretched from horizon to horizon and swayed in a sea of ripening harvest. This earth stood waiting for the plow. Waiting in vain. It would lie fallow this year, for its tillers were tilling city streets with their nails. That earth would not be seeded this year, for its sowers were seeding the streets of cities with their own bodies. This land would not bear a harvest this year. The harvesters themselves were being harvested by a grim reaper whose name is famine.

How deeply Andriy understood these people now, how near and dear they felt to him, even though, looking at outward appearances alone, there did not seem to be much of an affinity between them. Just very recently he, blind and arrogant, had tried to convince himself that he did not belong to this group, that he was different. But he was wrong. He was not different. He was a seed from the very same field, which only through some great miracle was able to jump out and find its way out of the mill of death and destruction. By a miracle! This did not give him the right to renounce his heritage. It did not give him the right, as *baba* had so aptly put it, to hide his head in the sand and to close himself off with lock and key away from the truth. On the contrary, he was obliged to look, to see, to remember. To remember in such a way so as to remember and not forget every single detail for the rest of his life!

Walking from the door of the factory to the tram stop, and from tram stop to the school door and then on the way home in the evening, Andriy paid close attention to the sight and the sound of each of these exiled, condemned people. In school, Andriy never ate his full ration of food. He always saved some of it to give to one of the starving. If he saw a dead body, he always stepped carefully around the body, and raised his hat in a sign of respect, making the sign of the cross over the body. He didn't care if anyone saw him doing this.

"Rest in Peace," he would whisper. "One day your soul will have a fitting memorial."

As a rule, Andriy came home late in the evenings, exhausted in body and in soul from the work, from school, and from the horrors witnessed along the way. He would wash up silently, change into comfortable clothes, and sit down to supper with Lidia Serhiyivna.

She understood him well and, feeling sorry for him, tried to cheer him up. She asked about school and work. He answered only in monotones. By comparison with what he was seeing on the city streets, the accomplishments at school or at work lost all significance.

"Everything is going well," he told her one day. "The foreman has drawn up a list of those who will receive an award and additional rations as a reward for good work and he put me on the list. Still, I would leave all of this behind and go back home. I am longing for the village, for the earth . . . . I am longing for it so much that I would even sign myself into a *kolhosp*. It makes no difference whether I work at the factory or in the *kolhosp*—in either case I will be a mere hireling."

Lidia Serhiyivna listened to him attentively and calmly, as always, and replied, "What is important here, Andriy, is neither the award nor the extra rations. What is important is that you are getting an education. When you finish trade school, you will be able to enroll in the workers' industrial school, and then be able to move on to an institute. You are now a citizen of 'the first category' and have a right to the privileges that come with that status. If you go back to the village where people and the authorities know you, you will revert back to being the son of a *kurkul.*"

"Do you think I'm a baby and don't understand this? I know this myself. It's one thing to want something, and quite another to actually do it. However, if I do go and study, I want only to become an agronomist. I'm unlikely to be able to ever go back to my own home, but working the land is a hundred times dearer to me than working in some factory. And peasants are nearer and dearer to me than factory workers. Only, by that time, I wonder if any of them will be left alive."

"They won't starve everyone, Andriy."

"May God hear you! Because it seems to me like there cannot be a living soul left in the villages. So many of them, so many, are dying here in the streets that . . . . Indeed, just as you say, I will have to suffer through all of this somehow. But it is not easy to suffer in this way. You were also right in saying so."

Andriy had no time to think too much, but from time to time he felt a pang of hurt feelings towards his adopted *baba.* It seemed that they were so close, so sincere and open with each other, and yet Lidia Serhiyivna never said anything about herself. What did he know about her? That she had a daughter named Tetiana, whose son he was supposed to be, and that her deceased husband had been a doctor and that they had had three children. That was it. So, her husband had died. But what happened to her children, to Tetiana, Andriy's "mother?" He should at least know that much. But Lidia Serhiyivna said nothing. That had to mean that she did not want him to know. Since she did not want him to know, it would not have been right to question her. That offended Andriy.

7

A month went by in this manner.

One day, as he waited in line at the tram stop, Andriy noticed a familiar comical figure. He had to think really hard to remember who it was—that fidgety boy he had once given two handfuls of barley. The boy had not changed a bit. He was dressed in the same drab peasant's overcoat and sheepskin hat, which kept inching down his forehead and onto his nose, and he was just as thin as before, and still looked like a straw toy-doll. The only thing new about him, which surprised Andriy, was the bundle of books and notebooks, strapped together, that he was carrying under his arm.

For some reason the sight of the boy made Andriy feel happy. Smiling, he poked him in the neck.

The boy whirled around, caught a glimpse of Andriy, took three steps back and, circling around him, kept looking at him as if upon something miraculous.

"Hmm," he said, scrutinizing him from all angles. "Seems you haven't been living badly at all."

"You're right," laughed Andriy in response. "And you, I see, have become a student, no?"

The boy pointed an index finger at himself.

"Ah yes. I have a *propyska* now and am a student at School No. 37."

"You don't say!" said Andriy, amazed. "How did you get so lucky?"

"By marrying off my grandmother. I found her a husband and a grandpa for myself. The *propyska*, ration cards, and the right to study were a result of the marriage."

Andriy looked at him with widened eyes.

"You've married off your grandmother?" he asked again, not believing his own ears. "You're lying!"

"No, I'm not."

"To whom?"

"Well, to that drunkard, who allowed us to live in his shed. I told you about him, didn't I?"

The tram was a long time coming, and the boy began telling his story.

"Oh, there was so much laughter. It all happened—well, I guess it'll be three weeks ago now. The old man, his name is Manchenko, had not come out of his house for two whole days. We knew he was home, since we saw him come in one night very drunk. So grandmother had me go and check up on him. She was worried he might have died from too much drink, and worried what would happen to us if he did. So I went. He was lying on the floor, moaning barely audibly. I went to him, helped him to sit up and to rest his back against the wall. I gave him some water and asked how he was feeling.

"He told me that two days earlier he had drunk so much that he almost died. I asked him why he drinks, pointing out that, if he continued in this way, he will surely kick the bucket soon. He gave me an incredibly mournful look, and replied, 'I don't care, son. I have a terminal illness, and I'm afraid of dying. That's why I drink.' 'If you are afraid of death, then don't drink, for the alcohol will kill you faster than the illness will,' I replied.

"He did not respond to this. Perhaps he didn't even hear me, for he went on, 'This life is terrible, and still one doesn't want to die. Here I am all alone. After I'm gone, there will be nobody to mourn me, not even a dog. Earlier, I lived here with my sister and her husband. They have two children. My sister and I own this house jointly. But when I started drinking, my sister and her family fled, preferring to live in rented quarters. And so I was left all alone. So, you see, I traded my whole family for whiskey. And now I am alone and even more afraid of death than before, and that's why I drink even more. Oh how I wish I had a shot of whiskey for this hangover right now!'

"I happened to have 70 whole rubles in my pocket from a wallet I managed to 'organize' from one of the passengers on the tram. So I said to him, 'I will get a full half-liter of whiskey, *diad'ku*, if you will only do what I ask of you.' 'Speak,' he said. 'Marry my grandmother. You will have a better life and so will we.'

"At first he did not want to. At one point he even seemed like he wanted to pick a fight, but he was too weak to move. He said that he hadn't married in his fifty years of life and that he would die single. 'Well,'

I responded, 'if you have decided to die, then nothing matters to you anymore anyway. But we—we still need to live. So do a last good deed now, just before you die. Besides, you will probably live longer if you have us to take care of you. I'll fetch the whiskey, grandma will cook some good food and make sure you have clean clothing. Marry her, please, I beg you humbly. You won't be sorry you did. My grandma is not a *kurkul*, only very poor. She even signed up into the *kolhosp*, and had given her cow and her plot of land to the state. The only problem was she was too old to do the amount of work they demanded on the *kolhosp*. She is able to keep up with housework, for the most part, but she is just not able to work in the fields.'

"He heard me out and then said, 'The hell with you and your grandmother. OK, I'll marry her! Only run now and get me that booze, because if I don't have a drink, I'll go mad. Besides, a marriage celebration calls for a drink!'"

Andriy listened and smiled, "What a little devil!" he thought. The tram came and they climbed in.

"What about your grandmother? What did she say?" asked Andriy.

"O-o-oof! She cried, and cried! If someone had heard her, they would have thought I was trying not to marry her off, but to bury her alive! Oh my, how she dressed me down. She nearly plucked all the hair off my head in anger. I nearly became as bald as Manchenko himself. 'You little devil!' she screamed. 'What have you dreamed up? I am a widow for twenty years now, and nobody could point a finger at me for unseemly behavior, and you would have me give up my respect and dignity and marry now? You want to make a laughing stock of me in my old age?'

"At this point, Manchenko unexpectedly took my side. 'Do not scold him, *Baba*,' he said. 'The idea of marrying is as difficult for me to accept as it must be for you, but we have this child to save. Though so young, he's managed to take care of you quite well. He's a courageous young boy, and I've grown to like him, though he is not my own. I can imagine that you feel even sorrier for him than I. Today, tomorrow, or the next day, I will die, and you will not even have this shed to live in. You'll perish, both of you. I'm not so sorry for you, for you have lived a long life. But what about him? What will he do? Join a gang of criminals?'

"He kept talking with my grandma, as I had talked to him. Finally, grandma settled down, still only saying that she's too old for him—a full twelve years older. To which he replied, 'I don't care a whit about that!

Even if you were one hundred years old, it would make no difference to me.'

"The only problem left was that my grandmother did not have the documents necessary to formalize a marriage," continued Hryts. "Manchenko had all his documents in order. So I quickly made all the arrangements for them to travel back to the village together, where all her records were, and to get married there. I even gave them 20 rubles for the road, making sure to give the money to her, to avoid giving Manchenko the opportunity to spend it on drink."

"And what?" asked Andriy, impatiently. "Did they marry?"

"Naturally. They got married in the village hall. And then they drank to celebrate the good bargain they had made!"

"So you are no longer living in the shed?"

"We're still in the shed because Manchenko still drinks, and the devil himself would not be able to tolerate living in the same house with him when he's drunk."

"He continues to drink?" asked Andriy.

"And how! It's true that he stayed sober for two whole days while he was taking all the necessary steps to register us and get the necessary documents for us. After that, he got so stinking drunk and drank for four days without stopping. He was in the grip of a desperately angry mood. We tried talking some sense into him, but that only enraged him further. 'I did not promise to stop drinking!' he roared. 'This is a time of emancipation: a woman knows her job, a man knows his. You are not going to stop me. If you keep after me, I'll divorce you. I'll go to the authorities immediately to sign a document appealing for divorce.' So we stopped bothering him. If he wants to drink, let him drink. We are happy to have the *propyska* and the ration cards. And grandma will even collect some kind of pension soon, based on the fact that she is unemployable and has an ailing husband. And I will get some privileges too, having the official status of a dependent now."

They had come to Andriy's stop, and he had to get off.

"Well, God be with you, then!" he said to Hryts.

"And with you!" replied the boy. "But come and visit us some day. We don't live very far away from you: 2 Ustymivskyj Lane. Only come to the shed, and not the house. Will you come?"

"I will try," promised Andriy, and began fighting his way to the door of the tram.

All day Andriy thought about this encounter. In the evening, when he told Lidia Serhiyivna about it, she laughed heartily. It was the very first time he had heard her laugh since he met her.

"Oh, that's so ingenious!" she exclaimed. "What a clever boy!"

She laughed again and added, "Someone like that will go far. Only who's to tell whether he will walk on the side of good or on the side of evil . . ."

Andriy suddenly felt a pang of jealousy and shame. Truly, that boy was such a little tyke, and yet he managed all on his own. Not only had he saved his own skin, but his grandmother's as well, while he, Andriy, would have perished if not for *baba*.

"True," he admitted gloomily. "Although I am older than he, I would not have been quick enough to manage like that!"

"People have different natures, Andriy," said Lidia Serhiyivna gently. "There are people who are flexible and people who are unbending. Do not be jealous of Hryts. Be the way you are, though life is oftentimes more difficult for people like you. Hold on to your pride, because it is in your blood. If you lose your pride, you will lose your own self. Remember that!"

She stepped up to him and, unexpectedly, kissed him on the forehead. With this kiss she broke down the final barriers between them, and wiped away the differences in social status, which Andriy always felt stood between him—a simple peasant boy, and her—this proud lady, who in poverty and in these lawless times nonetheless knew how to preserve her dignity and, even when peeling potatoes, did so with the innate majesty of a true princess.

Andriy restrained a desire to throw himself upon her breast and to shower her wrinkled cheeks with kisses and to express all of the feelings her unexpected caress had awakened in him. Instead, in an unconscious imitation of his benefactress, he simply got up and bowed his head.

"Thank you, *Baba!*" he responded quietly and solemnly.

8

That night, something terrible, unexpected and incomprehensible happened. Andriy was awakened in the middle of the night by lights, and the sound of men's voices coming from the other room. Disoriented, he sat up in bed, blinking. He looked around for a long time before he understood that there were two men in the house ordering Lidia Serhiyivna to get dressed and to come with them.

"Where are they taking you, *Baba*?" asked Andriy. "What do they want?"

"Keep quiet; don't ask any questions!" she ordered.

"And who is this?" asked one of the men, pointing to Andriy.

"My grandson," she retorted curtly. "Ten years I searched for him and finally found him a month and a half ago in an orphanage."

"Does he have a *propyska*?"

Lidia Serhiyivna brought out the registry and threw it on the table for the men to see for themselves. Then she went to change into street clothes, for she was still in her nightdress under the coat she had draped over her shoulders.

The uninvited guests began poring over the registry book, while Andriy looked at them more closely. He realized that they were operatives of the secret police and that they had come to arrest *baba*. One of them was quiet and restrained, had quite an intelligent but unpleasant face, an air of nonchalance about him, and sat on the edge of a chair scrutinizing his own nails. The other one, obviously the lower ranking of the two, had very broadly spaced yellowish-green eyes and a long thin nose. He was carefully measuring the walls with his gaze and constantly sniffing at something in the air. His dull face broke out in an idiotic smile from time to time, exposing a set of dark teeth.

Andriy sat motionless, though his heart beat wildly and his head was swimming with hundreds of questions. Why are they taking *baba*? What will they do with her? Are they taking her simply to interview her about something, or are they actually arresting her? What was he to do? Was he to defend her? To ask questions? Go with her? She had told him to remain silent and not to ask any questions. Why?

And what about that explanation she had given those men about him? He had a feeling that the comment was made more for his benefit than for theirs, so that he would know how to answer should anyone question him. Too bad, however, that she forgot to name the orphanage where she had supposedly found him.

How calm and dignified she was standing in the presence of those all-powerful goons! The situation must have been very difficult for her, but she did not let on at all. The only thing that betrayed her emotions was that her face was much paler than normal.

Now she stood at the threshold, dressed and ready.

"Bring all the letters with you," the quiet one reminded her.

"I have no letters," she replied icily. "And you know that very well."

"We know nothing, except . . ." interrupted the long-nosed one.

"Well then, the people who sent you know!" she snapped back at them unforgivingly, and then turned to Andriy.

"Andriy, do not be surprised. This is not the first time they have come for me."

"Talking is forbidden!" shouted the offended long-nosed officer in Russian.

Lidia Serhiyivna ignored him, and continued, "I will be back in a few days."

"Stop the talking!" raged the goon in an even more strident tone.

"Do not look for me and do not go anywhere!" continued Lidia Serhiyivna emphatically. "Do you understand? Go about your business at school and at work as you would normally, and say nothing to no one. Be smart. There is money in the drawer of the table."

She had managed to say what needed to be said, in spite of the fact that the second man pitched in to try to stop her.

"Enough, citizen! Let's go!" he shouted in Russian.

And she left. Without even saying "good-bye." But the look she gave him was so expressive that he clearly understood what she was trying to tell him. In the presence of such people it would be undignified to show any emotion at all. Fear, pain, hurt, anger—they all had to be squelched, and hidden under the guise of cool indifference. This was how she behaved and Andriy followed her lead. He returned her gaze calmly, not allowing even one muscle in his face to twitch and betray the deep emotions he was feeling. He stood immobile as a stone.

Only after the gate slammed shut, and the car had thundered away, did Andriy jump out into the street feeling as if he had been set on fire. He stood in the cold in his underwear for a few minutes, then went back in, put on his overcoat, and stepped outside again. He walked in and out in this way more than ten times, not really knowing why or what he was expecting to see. He wanted to scream, to call for help, or run after the *"chornyj voron"* (black raven) automobile. Finally, he came back in and slumped onto the couch without even turning off the lights, and fell into a fitful sleep. He woke only when the factory whistles sounded at 7:00 a.m. Then he got up and got ready for school. As he was leaving, he remembered the key. He came back to look for it, but could not find it; Lidia Serhiyivna had accidentally taken it with her.

The day went by in a kind of semi-fog. Every tool he picked up appeared to double in front of his eyes. Everything around him seemed surreal. Everything he did that day—working, eating, listening to lectures at school—he did mechanically. He came alive again only at the end of the day, when he exited through the iron gate. Home! Maybe *baba* was back already? Though she did say that she would be back in a few days, but maybe, just maybe . . . . Andriy hurried along, barely able to catch his breath in his hurry.

But the house was quiet and sad. It did not greet him with a friendly light peeping through the cracks in the window, or with a comforting stream of smoke curling up from the chimney. The gate, which had been left unlocked, had been torn loose from the lock by the wind, and was swinging back and forth, clanging steel against steel.

Inside the house, Andriy was greeted with a gust of cold air. Everything was in disarray, and there was a depressing feeling of emptiness in the house—the kind of emptiness one feels after a death in the family has occurred.

Andriy took an axe to cut some kindling for the fire, but then changed his mind. He lay down on the couch again in all his clothes and fell into a deep dead sleep.

He woke up cold but refreshed, despite the fact that even in sleep he was aware of the misfortune that had fallen on him and his *baba*, for it all came back to him the minute he opened his eyes. Not knowing what time it was, he stepped out into the street. Judging from the activity in the street, and the number of people standing at the public water tap already, he guessed that it must be about six o'clock.

He made a fire, tidied up the house, cooked breakfast, washed up, ate and left. His spirits were fortified by the good night's sleep and by the warm breakfast, and he began to feel hopeful that *baba* would indeed come back. She had said that this was not the first time they had come for her. Why did they take her? Why?

The next four days Andriy's spirits had lifted a bit. He had started praying again before breakfast—a habit he had sorely neglected during his wanderings. He left the house every morning believing that he would find *baba* back at home when he returned in the evening. But he was bitterly disappointed every night. The house stood dark and cold, and emptiness and quiet reigned inside.

Life went on. The students working at the factory were relieved of their duties there. Someone somewhere in the government suddenly remembered the child labor laws in effect. An announcement was made that this was to be the students' last day at work. A meeting was called. The secretary of the local Komsomol group gave an hour-long speech about what a joyous life youth in the Soviet Union had. He spoke a great deal about the Party and about the government and of their paternal care for the country's youth, and about how young people did not have such care in any capitalist country in the world. He ended with the thought that, though young people were eagerly chomping at the bit to help the Party and the country and begging to be allowed to work despite their young years, the Party and the government had to disappoint them and not allow them to do so in the interest of their health, which was the most important concern to all Party and government officials. He expressed the hope that the students would transfer all of their energy into their schoolwork and into learning their professions well.

Speeches by other Party members and Komsomol workers followed, and the meeting stretched out for two long hours. It ended with the handing out of awards and extra rations to the most deserving workers and students. All the master craftsmen, some of the workers, and a small number of students—Andriy among them—were the recipients. The rest had to content themselves with flowery expressions of thanks and of gratitude from the Party and the government.

Andriy's prize was half a liter of cooking oil, a kilo of black bread, two kilos of millet, half a kilo of sugar and 12 *karbovantsi* (dollars in Ukrainian currency). He almost had to leave the oil behind, for he had nothing he could pour his share into. Only when one of the workers gave him an empty liquor bottle was Andriy able to pour out his share of the precious liquid into it.

That night, Andriy came back to the house a rich man. In addition to the booty he had been awarded at the factory, he had also received his stipend at school that afternoon. So he had a bagful of food and 50 karbovantsi! He walked home feeling certain that he would find his *baba* at home. She just had to be there! She had to! It was not possible that she would not be there to share in his great good luck that day!

Alas, Lidia Serhiyivna had not returned, and Andriy's mood plummeted to a new low. He thrust everything on the table, and sat down gloomily, cradling his head in his hands. How will it be? How much longer can they keep the poor woman? Perhaps it would be better not to heed her commands and start making inquiries about her whereabouts? Maybe she needs a care package? He could start right after the weekend. And then he thought—well, she might still come back tonight. This was a possibility yet, for those vipers never take or return anybody during the day, but only under cover of night. Just like werewolves. That's probably what they will do with *baba* as well. They took her at night, and will bring her back at night as well. If that's the case, Andriy was determined that she should return to find a warm home and something warm to eat.

Deluding himself with this spark of hope, Andriy busied himself around the house. He chopped some kindling for the fire and lit it. Busy, he did not hear the gate creak open, and was terribly startled by a knock on the door. Something in his chest jumped with gladness as he rushed to the door.

"*Ba . . .*!" he shouted, flinging the door open, and stopped short.

There was an old woman standing at the threshold, but it was not the one he was so eagerly awaiting. Dressed in a sheepskin coat, a thick, dot-covered shawl that was wrapped from her head to her knees, boots, and holding a walking stick, the woman said "hello" and, without asking permission, stepped over the threshold, stamped her feet to loosen the snow off her boots and, unasked and unbidden, made her way to the kitchen, sitting down on the bench there.

"They took the doctor's wife again? Poor thing!" she sighed sadly. Her words were neither a question nor a statement.

"Whom are you looking for?" asked Andriy in a none-too-friendly tone. "I'm asking about the doctor's wife," she answered, not at all offended. "I came to visit you. Do you know me?"

"This is the first time I have ever seen you," replied Andriy, in the same unpleasant tone as before.

"Ah, but I see you every day through my window," she answered peaceably. "My name is Mrs. Nestorenchuk, and people refer to me simply as *Baba* Nastya (short for Anastasia). Our house is on the other side of the street facing the public water tap, where you go to fetch water. I heard that they've taken the doctor's wife, and thought to myself: 'I'll go to that poor orphan and have a word with him and comfort him.' I see that you have been left here all alone, and you are not from here, as one can see. The doctor's wife has given you lodging, has she, or what?"

The woman appeared sincere, and a good person, but she was excessively inquisitive.

"I'm her grandson!" replied Andriy angrily and not very convincingly.

The visitor smiled with only the corners of her aged mouth and only sighed.

"If you are her grandson, then so be it!" she agreed.

"Only I knew this woman and her deceased husband, the doctor (may he rest in peace!) long before you were born. I knew all of her children."

Noticing Andriy's surprised and mistrustful expression, the lady nodded her head and continued:

"I worked for six years as their cook, so how could I not know? Besides, everybody in Kharkiv knew Dr. Cherniavsky. His reputation spread even beyond Kharkiv. He was the best! He was a doctor like no other. He was not one of those who split the world into lords and common folk. Whoever was sickest and needed his help the most—that's who got his attention first. Dr. Cherniavsky would leave the governor himself waiting to go and save some farmer who needed his help out in the hinterlands somewhere. He was so rich, such a lord, that he kept five servants. He never shunned or kept his distance from simple folk. And he spoke our language so well that one would think that he had been born in a village and that Ukrainian was the only language he was fluent in. His wife, Lidia Serhiyivna, was the same way. If ever anyone called her '*baryshnia,*' (Miss in Russian) she would cut them to pieces with her angry sarcasm. 'What is the matter with you?' she would say. 'Don't you know your own language?' She was a great supporter of an independent Ukraine from way back—even back during Tsarist times. Others would have been exiled and sent off to Siberia for holding such views. But not the Cherniavskys. He was too great a doctor, he was!"

The woman fell silent, deep in thought, shaking her head sadly.

"The world is strange sometimes. Some people kill and slaughter without regard for anything, and another saves his fiercest enemies from death. Take Dr. Cherniavsky, for example. Obviously, he needed that Communist Party as much as we need collectivization. However, when the Revolution came, they took him to some Red hospital to tend to those antichrists. And he did. They say he saved one of the highest ranking People's Commissars, I forgot what his name was, from certain death. They say that the man rewarded him with something that protected him from all future assaults. The man certified that Cherniavsky was a genuine 'Communist doctor' and that no one has the right to molest him in any way. Unfortunately, this did not save him from typhoid fever. When the plague struck, it did not ask who was Red and who White. Just like the good doctor—he only saw that a person was sick, and did not care whether that sick person was a Christian or a Communist antichrist. He tended to his patients until he himself contracted typhoid fever and died shortly thereafter.

Andriy listened attentively, not wanting to miss a word. But suddenly, the visitor fell silent. Shaking her head, she wiped the corners of her mouth with a handkerchief.

"Ha!" she continued. "In the end, it probably turned out better for him that way. Commendations or no commendations, they would have killed him sooner or later, like they did all the rich folk. And they would have killed her, too. But that Commissar's testimony on behalf of Cherniavsky bought her time. It kept her safe during the first wave of terror, when the killing and slaughter was at its worst. After a while, the storm abated, and they stopped persecuting the educated class quite as much as they had in the past. They still went after the generals and the wealthy, and some merchants. But they started leaving the doctors and the teachers and the in . . . in . . . How do you call those people who build roads and bridges?"

"Engineers?"

"Yes, yes! Injineers! They started putting those people back to work, for those Communists were mostly uneducated and illiterate people, people who were barely capable of signing their names. They gave Lidia Serhiyivna some kind of a job in a hospital. But they took away her home, the one she and the doctor had lived in together on Sumska Street, and resettled her in this shanty. At least they did not throw her out into the street, like they did most others. She worked for three years in that hospital, and then I don't know what happened, whether they let her go or whether she quit. But since then she has been here at home. She has some kind of pension. This I know for certain, for we both go and pick up our money at the Social Security office. But naturally, you know all of this already, for she has told you all about it herself."

Andriy knew nothing of any of this, but he was too ashamed to admit it. So he lied, lamely and none too convincingly, again, "Well, yes, she did tell me a few things."

"Oh, she's not one of those who like to talk!" picked up *Baba* Nastya, noting Andriy's confusion. "She was born proud, that woman was. It's not that she is bad or conceited or anything, just . . . well, just proud. When they resettled her here, her demeanor was even prouder than before. You see, stupider folk quickly put on airs when they come into a bit of riches; others, who go from rich to poor, do not fold. They still hold on to their dignity. Lidia Serhiyivna is one of those. She's polite and always greets others with a '*Dobryj den!*' (Good morning!) or a '*Daj Bozhe zdorovlia!*'

(May God grant you good health!), but that is it. She does not stop to talk or socialize with anyone. I don't know whether it's because she is angry, or because she feels offended. Whatever it is, she speaks with no one, despite the fact that many people know her here.

"It's hard for her. She was such a great lady, and now she has to carry her own water and cut down her own wood for the stove, and paint her own house, and do the garden work—all by herself. At first, people wanted to help her. She thanked them, and refused. Only once when they put in the water posts on the streets, and ordered everybody to cover up their wells, did she ask a neighbor who owned a nag and a cart to bring in some soil. Two weeks he was carting soil to her house from some ravine. She paid him and that was that. That's how she is! I would have never come by if she were here alone. Why trouble someone against her wishes? But, you see, I did come to see you. I feel sorry for her and I feel sorry for you. But don't say anything to her."

Mrs. Nestorenchuk suddenly bent down closer to him and whispered in his ear, "This is the third time they have come for her. It's because of the gold."

Andriy jumped back, thinking that perhaps the woman was not quite right in her mind.

"Because of what?" he asked.

"I'm telling you, it's because of the gold," she repeated, somewhat louder.

"What gold?"

"What do you mean 'what gold?' The gold! Many people are now suffering because of gold."

Andriy kept looking at her with wide eyes, uncomprehending.

"You see," smiled Mrs. Nestorenchuk, "one can see immediately that you are not from the city, if you know nothing about this. Let me explain. The secret police have a way of sniffing out that someone has gold held over from tsarist times. It could be just a matter of jewelry—rings, gold earrings with precious stones or gems. Once they know, they seize the person and order them to hand over these valuables to the government. The more easily frightened people just hand it over right away, not waiting until they begin to torture them."

"Torture them?" repeated Andriy becoming white as a sheet.

Noticing Andriy's shock, the woman immediately corrected herself.

"Well, perhaps not so much "torture" as they try to scare a person into doing what they want," she said, trying to put things a bit more mildly. "You know, they say, 'Unless you give us your gold, you will never leave here: we may even exile you to Siberia.' I have never heard of a case where they actually did not let somebody go. Even the staunchest among them return home after a week or ten days. But one never knows. There's no joking around with these people. They say they will not release you and sometimes they don't. People have no recourse. What can they do? People who really don't have any gold or valuables are the worst off. Someone, motivated by jealousy or envy, tips off the authorities, and the person is made to suffer.

"Take the case of Lidia Serhiyivna. During the revolution, they robbed her of everything. They even took her furniture. What they didn't take, they broke. What you see here is all she has left. She had so many beautiful things, she really did! And . . . ," again Mrs. Nestorenchuk bent over towards him, lowering her voice, "there's no point in hiding the truth, they did have a lot of gold. And Lidia Serhiyivna had a lot of beautiful jewelry. She had so much that it would be difficult to keep count of everything. She had rings and earrings and bracelets and necklaces—Lord! If I hadn't seen them with my own eyes, I would never have believed it. Everything was made of gold and with beautiful sparkling gems. That's what they were after, those barefoot tramps who carried out the revolution. That's why they joined! They stole, looted and even killed in the process. They didn't kill Lidia Serhiyivna because of her husband. But they stole all her valuables just the same. They took it all, every single piece. Even that piece of paper from the Commissar was not able to shield her from that."

"So why are they picking on her now?" said Andriy, more to himself than to Mrs. Nestorenchuk, and immediately got angry. He continued in his thoughts. "Why are they bothering her? Why did they bother my father with taxes when they knew very well there was not a single kernel of wheat in the house, when it was evident to all that the whole family was swelling from starvation! Why did they bother everybody else? Dragged them, night after night, to village halls, humiliated them and beat them!"

"Son, they go after everyone, may they never have any peace!" replied Mrs. Nestorenchuk, expressing aloud what Andriy was thinking. "And they bother Lidia Serhiyivna also on account of her children. You see, she had three children, two of them currently living abroad:

a daughter and a son. The oldest daughter became a Sister of Mercy and went to the battlefront, never to be heard from again. The two younger ones live in France somewhere. They write to Lidia Serhiyivna and send her money through *Torgsin* (from the Russian '*Torgovlia s inostrantsiami*'—trade with foreigners). The mailman himself always said that Lidia Serhiyivna must have been born lucky. In Tsarist times, she literally bathed in gold, and now she lives on money she gets from abroad. He would always say, 'I deliver letter after letter to her from *Torgsin*.'"

"What did you say?" Andriy didn't understand. "Torg . . . ? What is that?"

"So, you don't even know that?" said the surprised woman. "They opened a store called *Torgsin* which is stocked with everything, just as if we were still living in Tsarist times, and even better than in Tsarist times. Only, you can't buy anything there with our Soviet money. Just foreign currency, gold, or precious stones can be used. First one purchases something called *bony* (certificates) and these *bony* can be used to purchase anything in the store. Only they are cunning little foxes. Under the tsar, five gold rubles would have bought you a whole bag of the finest rye flour. Now, you can't even get half a bag of ordinary flour for that amount. Everywhere you go, there is price gouging and thievery. That's the kind of government we have now!"

"Somehow, I don't believe in this story about *baba* having foreign currency," said Andriy. "*Baba* was living on near-starvation rations. All that's left in her cellar are maybe two pails of potatoes, about twenty carrots, and perhaps half a bag of dried pears—all of which she had harvested herself from the garden. She told me that the dried pears are from her own tree too. She used to trade clothes for barley to make some kind of barley broth for me to eat while I was ill and did not have any ration cards. And even now, although I now have ration cards, we never eat until we are full. I simply do not believe that she could possibly have any *bony*."

"Well, my dear, this is something I know nothing about," replied Mrs. Nestorenchuk, disappointed. "I am only telling you what I have heard. So, where is it that you work?"

"I am studying metalworking at the Trade School. We work half a day, and attend all kinds of lectures the other half. Most of our time is spent reading Marx and Engels," said Andriy in a derisive tone.

102

"Thank God for that!" said Mrs. Nestorenchuk in a moralizing tone. "Much better than being out there with the criminal element, or standing with outstretched hand, begging . . . . Well, let me leave. Stay well."

"Don't go, auntie," begged Andriy. "I'll cook some millet, and we'll have dinner together."

"Go ahead and cook, son. But these are not the times for inviting guests to stay for dinner."

Andriy did not want to be alone, and alternatively begged and insisted that she stay, saying he would not eat at all tonight if left on his own and without company.

"All right, then, I'll stay. Give me what you were going to cook and I will make dinner for us."

She took off her overcoat, pulled up her sleeves, and started to cook supper. She would not let Andriy help. She lit the fire herself, rinsed the millet, peeled two potatoes and a carrot. Putting them in a pot of water to cook, she sat down to talk.

Mrs. Nestorenchuk was a very talkative person. She told Andriy about herself, about her family, where they came from. She told him about her daughter and her son-in-law, with whom she lived and with whom she did not get on very well, and about her disobedient grandchildren. She told him that the best time in her life had been when she had worked for the Cherniavskys. There was plenty to eat and drink, she had nothing to worry about, she saved her money, and would even get a whole new wardrobe at Easter and Christmas. She was plump then, and very well dressed. She recounted with great satisfaction the recipes she used to cook to perfection, and how she was able to satisfy the special tastes of each member of the family. She talked about the Cherniavsky children, too, and about their characters. There was Tanya, quiet and serious, her dad's favorite child, who from early childhood had dreamed of becoming a doctor. Then there was Vera—bubbly and fidgety, who loved to dance more than anything else in the world, and was always twirling in front of the mirror. Finally, Borys, a very determined child who, influenced by books he had read, was fixated on finding treasure under the old pear tree in their garden overlooking the Lopan' River.

"Days on end he would be under that pear tree," smiled Mrs. Nestorenchuk. "He shoveled and shoveled until his hands were covered in calluses. But he never got very far. The earth underneath that tree was dense and hard and full of roots. Even a strong peasant would have had difficulty digging much of a hole there. But no matter what people said, he insisted on digging underneath that pear tree."

Mrs. Nestorenchuk got up from time to time to stir the thick soup and to taste it. Then she sat back down again and talked some more. By the time they finally sat down to dinner, she tried to pry information out of Andriy in every way possible, but he held his tongue firmly and did not fall into the many traps she set. He firmly ignored her questions, and just as firmly remained silent and made no comment on the numerous conjectures that peppered her conversation. At one point, she even got mad at his restraint. She had told him so many things and she felt she had a right to learn a few things from him. But Andriy stubbornly refused to trust her and talk openly in front of her.

Only after she had washed the dishes and put on her coat to leave, he asked, "*Titko* (auntie), do you have any idea where I could look for *baba*?"

Mrs. Nestorenchuk nearly jumped up, perturbed at the question.

"No, my dear, I do not know. And you don't need to know either. You can get into a lot of trouble if you go looking for her. You could make the situation a whole lot worse for her. The secret police will not just take your word that you are really her grandson, and they'll start questioning you. And, furthermore, dear, you will not get away with telling them pretty stories about a spotted bull, nor will they allow you to hold your tongue as you do with me. There, you will be forced to tell them the whole truth. Then . . . . Well, you yourself must know how things would end up."

Having thus vented her anger at Andriy's silence in this way, Mrs. Nestorenchuk finished on a gentler note:

"May God protect you, son, for you are a good child. Don't try to look for your *baba*, as you call her. They will let her go, you'll see. If you need anything, or if you just want to come and visit, do so. Y'a hear?"

They said goodbye to each other and she left.

Andriy felt a bit better. He wasn't sure whether it was because it had been a comfort to have someone to talk with or because he was relieved to be rid of so inquisitive a person. Still, he had learned many valuable things from her, things that he had really yearned to know. This both worried him and made him feel more at peace. Most of all, however, he realized how extremely tired he was. His brain, and his body, cried out for rest. Sleep! Sleep!

9

The next day, Andriy, on a whim, decided to visit Hryts. Winter was coming to an end and it was sunny and bright outside. By contrast, Lidia Serhiyivna's house felt gloomier and emptier than ever. The heavy weight that had lodged itself in his heart made it difficult for Andriy to be at peace in the house. That's why he decided to go out.

Andriy found his way to the house on Ustymivskyj Lane, and knocked on the gate. He heard the sound of a door opening, and of footsteps crunching on the snow.

A familiar voice called out, "Who's there?"

"It's me—Andriy. Remember me?"

"Of course I remember you. But I'd no idea until this very minute that your name is Andriy."

Hryts swung open the gate, and Andriy peered at him closely. He looked different—glum, and unlike his normal self.

"Come in," said Hryts, inviting Andriy in.

Stepping over the threshold, Andriy caught sight of a lady's face for a second in a window of the house across the way, and then it disappeared very quickly.

"Was that your grandmother?" asked Andriy, cocking his head in the direction of the window.

"No. She's the sister of the deceased Manchenko."

"Deceased?" Andriy shuddered. "But, you . . . only recently . . ."

"Indeed—*recently!* Turns out he was already dead that day we met, only I didn't know it yet. When I left the house in the morning, grandmother and I thought he was just in one of his drunken stupors. As it turned out, though, he had surrendered his spirit to God for real that time. So you see, my grandmother did not have to bemoan her tarnished reputation for very long. She's a widow once again."

Hryts's feeble attempt at humor fell flat. Looking at Hryts, Andriy thought that this day was an unfortunate one for both of them.

"Whom has God brought to the door?" called an old voice from inside the shed. An old woman was sitting at the window, needle in hand, mending an embroidered shirt.

"It's the boy who saved you from starving to death, grandma," replied Hryts.

"Stop making things up!" said Andriy, embarrassed at being cast in such an important role. He greeted the woman.

"I'm not making it up!" insisted Hryts. "If you don't believe me, ask grandma."

"Yes, for once he's telling the truth," said the old lady. "If it hadn't been for the hot soup he made with the barley you gave him, I surely would have been stiff as a board by morning, and not even the warmth of the down comforter would have helped me. For it's really true what people say: it's not the coat that warms the body, but the body that warms the coat. You can throw a down comforter, a sheepskin coat, or whatever, over a corpse, but you will not be able to warm it up. That day, I was so weak from hunger that I was truly half-dead already."

"I got a big scare when I got back home," cut in Hryts. "I touched her and she was so cold! I said something to her, but she just couldn't answer, and only moved her eyes from side to side. I quickly put the barley in a pot of water to cook and ran out to buy the smallest bottle of whisky I could find."

"He made me tipsy, that rascal did," added the woman, smiling.

"Made you tipsy?!" shot back Hryts, suddenly irritated. "I was barely able to force two spoonfuls of the stuff down your throat. Since I had to force the spoon into her mouth, I must have spilled at least half of the whiskey in the process. I was terrified you would die before the barley was soft enough to eat."

"Enough now!" said the lady, setting her sewing aside. "Ask your guest into our 'house,'" she continued, placing a mockingly bitter emphasis on the last word.

The shed was not very old. It was solidly built, and made of good wood, and even had a ceiling made of plywood. It was clear, however, that it had to be freezing inside when the weather was cold outside. Even today, though the snow outside was thawing and water was dripping from rooftops all around, there were still pockets of ice glistening on the uneven earthen floor.

Hryts had not lied about his circumstances that first time he met Andriy. Everything was exactly as he had described. There was the old wooden bed, spread with an old down comforter, a primus stove stood on a stool, a large can of kerosene and a tin pail full of water stood in the corner, and an aluminum pot was hanging from a nail on the wall. That was all there was.

But Hryts's grandmother looked completely different from the way in which Andriy had imagined her. She must have revived quite a bit on the ration cards they had recently received, for she was not only able to walk, but did so with a lively gait, and her face, although much too wrinkled and worn-out for her years, was the face of an energetic, witty, and very good woman. It was clear that she loved her grandson very much, but she kept him on a short leash, and Hryts was a bit afraid of her.

She had Andriy sit down on the bed, took out a bag of sunflower seeds, and offered some to him.

"Forgive us, son. This is all we have to offer you. But, '*Chym khata bahata tym rada*' (*With whatever our house is rich—we are ready to share with our guests*)."

"Thank you," smiled Andriy. "This is perfect. I haven't eaten sunflower seeds for a very long time, and I love them dearly."

Grandmother gave a handful to Hryts too, but he grimaced and complained.

"This is the second day in a row that you are feeding me sunflower seeds. You'd think I was a rooster. Soon, I'll grow a pip on my tongue!"

"Don't lie, lad, for you also have a slice of bread daily, and as much water as you can drink. Isn't that enough for you?"

"I want something hot to eat!" he replied capriciously.

"Lots of people want many things," replied his grandmother, sighing. "But, if it's not there to have, you have to do without."

"Well, I'll make it possible!" retorted Hryts, jumping up. "I will heat up the stove and cook my friend here a decent meal of barley soup."

Andriy said to them that they should not go to any trouble over him, but they were too distracted to hear him. The elderly woman had grabbed her grandson by the arm and was forcing him to sit back down.

"You will not heat anything up, Hryts!" she said sternly. "You should be ashamed of yourself! You are too big a boy to be acting like a child."

"Ashamed, ashamed," mimicked Hryts with tears of rage in his eyes. "Why don't you tell that witch that she ought to be ashamed and stop giving us such a hard time? Aha! You're scared of her!"

"You are being stupid, Hryts!" replied the woman calmly. "She's the landlady here. As such, she needs to be respected."

"Are you talking about the woman I saw peering out the window?" asked Andriy.

"Yes, yes, that damned woman, grandma's sister-in-law. Ouch!" he cried, as his grandmother pulled on his hair.

"I have told you already, you rascal," continued grandmother, tugging at his hair, "that she is not any sister-in-law of mine. My wedding day was forty-two years ago when I married your grandfather. We exchanged our vows in a church and in the presence of a priest and the angels up above. And from that day onward, I have been Mykolaikha Hrechaniuchka. This is the name I will die with. I have no intention of duping God with what those two dunces at the village hall scribbled down about me and Manchenko—may he find peace in heaven! I have no sister-in-law here! No, I really do not! And that is final!"

She kept tugging at her grandson's hair, while he kept trying to pull away, screaming, "Let go, grandma! Let go! It hurts . . . Ouch!"

"I don't understand," cut in Andriy in an effort to help Hryts out. "She's not allowing you to put the stove on, or what?"

"Not only does she not allow us to light the stove," complained Hryts, "she doesn't even allow us to turn on the lamp either! She says we could cause a fire. All winter we cooked and turned on the light, and nothing happened, and now . . . ."

"We used to light the fire because Manchenko had nothing against us doing so," said grandmother. "But his sister is the owner now, and she has other ideas. We'll have to get by without it. That's all there is to it."

"You might as well come out with the whole truth already, grandma!" shouted Hryts impatiently, turning to Andriy. "She's throwing us out, that's what! She wants us to give back the down comforter and the bed. She's only letting us keep the kerosene stove."

"And that is her right," said Hrechaniuchka firmly. "There's an old saying: 'if you don't own the cart, be prepared to get off midway through the journey.' Don't you understand that?"

The whole story poured out then, Hryts and his grandmother competing with each other to tell it all. Andriy found out about the whole drama and all the details. This is how it went . . . . Natalka Kuzmenko, Manchenko's sister, asked them to give back the keys to the house on the very day of Manchenko's funeral. She said she did not want to have any strangers living on the property. Her father had built the house, and had willed it to her and to her brother. They had lived here together until Manchenko started drinking and behaving badly. That's when she and her family moved out to rented quarters. Now, they wanted to come back home, and leave the rented house for their son, who was getting ready to marry soon.

"She does not have the right to throw you out," said Andriy.

"After all, you are officially registered at this address and have a *propyska*."

"Yes, that's true. We do have a *propyska*, but she is the rightful owner," said the elderly woman firmly.

"And where shall we go?" asked Hryts, fidgeting.

"That, my boy, is not her problem. Each person has to take care of himself."

"All right, I will take care of myself! I am not leaving here and that's that! What's more, next winter I'll put in an additional heater, I'll cut the wall to install a window, and I'll paint the walls. You'll see!"

"On somebody else's property?"

"Somebody else's property?!" retorted Hryts getting angrier still. "If she is going to do things to spite us, I will do the same to her!"

"Hryts, listen to me! She is not doing anything to spite us. We are uninvited guests here. We have come here unbidden. You do not yet understand how painful it is when strangers take what is rightfully yours and what has been in your family from generation to generation, and behave as if your property is their own. Is it any wonder that Herasym Shchuka took an axe and killed Sashko Kudlaty because he had robbed him of his land? Even the knowledge that he would certainly be sentenced to death for this deed did not stop him."

"But, *Baba* Mykolaikha," remonstrated Andriy. "This situation is a bit different. You did not force your way in here. Didn't Manchenko let you live here? Yes, he did. Didn't he go through the trouble of getting you registered here? Yes, he did. It is not your fault that he died. That woman should be grateful you are not trying to take full advantage of your legal rights."

"I, lad, live by my own code of honor," replied Hryts's grandmother, offended. "A code I had been taught as a child, one which is in accordance with God's will."

It was no use arguing with her any further. Manchenko's sister had given them two weeks to vacate the premises. Twelve days were left before they had to leave. Hryts's grandmother was determined to leave on the designated day, or even earlier, if she managed to get the passport she was waiting for and which she thought would be ready in another week. She had some vague hopes of moving to another city, where it would be easier to find a place to live and where she could look for a job to supplement the pension she had received from Manchenko ("May he rest in peace with the Lord, he was a good man," she said repeatedly). That's how she planned for them to live.

But Hryts, though young, was much more practical and sober about their prospects. It's easy to say—go to another city! But how will they go? They had no money for train tickets. Would they walk? That would take days. What would they eat before they were able to register in the new place? Where would they sleep? How would they survive until Manchenko's pension was mailed to them from Kharkiv to "this other place?" Would he, Hryts, have to resort to stealing once again? No, no, he thought, I don't want to have to do that again. At the very least, they must wait until summer. For even though the weather is mild today and it feels like winter is over, it could turn bitterly cold again tomorrow. He had had a taste of being out in the cold that was enough to last him a lifetime. He did not want to risk being in that situation again, especially not with an elderly woman in tow. His grandmother was far from strong. She could die on the road. If she did, he might as well just die along with her. What would he have to live for, all alone in the world!

Listening to his new acquaintances, Andriy forgot all about his own problems. He really liked Hryts's grandmother. Stubborn and inflexible though she was, she was an honest woman. He also really liked Hryts. Though he looked like such a little firebrand and rogue on the outside, what a warm and tender grandson he was!

Andriy had come to a decision. He didn't quite know what he would do, or how, but he got up and silently walked out of the shed.

"Where are you going? What for? Wait!"

He either did not hear these cries, or pretended not to. He walked briskly across the garden, bolted up the four front steps and entered the house. He walked through a hall, past the kitchen with its half-broken stove, past another room with walls that showed the brick under the peeling paint, and stopped on the threshold of the second room. Inside, a woman, all splattered in white whitewash, was perched on top of a table. She was painting the wall with such determination that she failed to notice the arrival of the visitor.

"Good morning, *titka* (auntie)," he greeted her politely.

The woman was so startled that she jumped and nearly spilled the pail of paint. She cursed and shot an angry look at Andriy.

"What do you want?"

"I wished you a good morning," repeated Andriy calmly, though he felt his voice harden.

"I heard you!" she fired back. "And I ask you again: what do you want?"

"Well, if you heard me, you should answer me first and only then ask me what I want."

"Listen to him! And where did you get to be so learned?"

"I'm not at all learned. But, at home, I was always taught that, if someone bids me 'good morning,' I should respond with 'May God grant you health'. Do you do things differently here?" Andriy responded with complete composure.

"Did you come here to preach to me?" cried the woman, jumping down from the table, and moving towards him menacingly. "Get out of my house!"

Andriy stood as if rooted to the ground, and boldly looked her in the eye.

"I could very well be the one saying that to you," he said quietly. "But . . . ."

"And what kind of a rare bird are you?" she said, enraged.

"I'm a person, not a bird, and again I say to you: good morning, *titka*."

"And I say: get out of here, before I slam this paintbrush into your face."

And she almost succeeded in doing just that, but Andriy caught her hand in the nick of time.

"Slow down, *titka*, slow down!" he said in a deathly quiet voice, turning pale. "If it comes down to using force, I will hurl you out into the street with such force—with the paint, the brush, and all your belongings—that it won't be easy to pick up the pieces."

Feeling his anger and strength, the woman stepped back, and angrily threw the brush to the floor, splattering paint all over.

"What a turn life has taken these days! A devil-knows-who finds his way into your home, and there's no recourse!"

"My right to be in this house is the same as yours, *titka*," continued Andriy in the same quiet but firm tone. "By which I mean—no right at all. For neither you nor I are legally registered here. You have as much right to throw me out as I have to throw you out!"

The woman cursed again, shouting, "You are comparing yourself to me? This house is mine!"

"It can be yours a hundred times over, but you are not registered as a legal resident here. Until your sister-in-law gives you the registry book to allow you to sign yourself in as a legal resident here, you have no authority."

The woman laughed a high-pitched, cynical laugh and replied, "That's a good one! As if I would ever ask that stray for any kind of permission! The registry book and the keys are in my possession already. There's nothing more she can do."

"Ah, so you've stooped to thievery or have resorted to violence! I'm afraid there's no other way but to call the police. Then we'll see who can and cannot do what to whom."

Andriy said this so firmly and threateningly that Natalia Kuzmenko went pale and was evidently at a loss.

"So, is this what you came for?" she asked, her voice saturated with hatred.

"No, *titka*. I came to you with a good word," replied Andriy sadly. "If you like, we can start all over again. I will bow to you again and say: God help us!"

"There is no God anymore!" she screamed, almost hysterically.

A look of surprise bordering on fear appeared on Andriy's face, which progressively changed into a bitterly sad smile on his almost imperceptibly warped lips.

"Well then, excuse me, Comrade Kuzmenko," Andriy replied, speaking slowly and gazing intently at the woman who seemed to shrink from shame. "If God does not exist for you, then let us speak as if He really doesn't exist. And so, you will go immediately to your sister-in-law and give her back the key and the registry book. As for the house, if you want to get your half of it, then you will have to file a claim with the court. Until the court reaches a decision, however, you must not dare show your face around here. Understood?"

The woman suddenly broke down in tears.

"So that's how it is?" she lamented, wiping her eyes on her apron. "You start out talking about God and end by throwing me out of my family home?"

"I wanted only to show how things are when people act without reference to God. You've fallen upon these honest people and you want to gobble them up alive. If Mrs. Hrechaniuk was like you, she would have taken a broom to you and shooed you off the grounds. She was legally married to your brother and is left a widow after his death, and she is legally registered here and she should have been living in this house a long time ago, rather than in that shed!"

"There's no truth in the world anymore! No more! God has forsaken us and turned His face away," lamented the woman.

"Oh!" said Andriy, surprised. "But you just said that there is no God. Why are you complaining now?"

"Ehh! Tongues often wag with thoughtless words. If I really did not have God in my soul, the situation would never have gotten to this point. I wanted to do everything the right way.

"When my brother, Vasyl, became ill, and started to drink and behave outrageously, people advised me to go to the police and file a report. Let them take him somewhere—to jail or to a sanatorium—anywhere, but get him out of the house. But I did not listen. How could I call the police on my own brother, one who was terminally ill, no less!

"But it was impossible to live with him. He did not let anyone sleep, and he scared the children half to death. That's why my husband and I decided to move away. We thought we'd let him live out however long God willed in this house, and we'd come back after he died. And then we got wind that Vasyl' had let some starving people live in the shed. My son came by to have a look. He came back and said it was true, and that Vasyl' had even given the people a bed and a down comforter. These things were a part of the dowry our mother had brought into her marriage.

"Again people warned us we would have trouble. They said Vasyl' was not in his right mind, and the authorities could take the house away from us because he allowed illegal residents to live here. Again we ignored the warnings, neither going to the police nor bothering the old woman and her grandson. We thought, if push came to shove, we could say that we knew nothing and saw nothing. We would explain that my brother was mentally not fully competent, being either drunk or in a daze most of the time, and that he probably did not even know that someone had broken into the shed.

"Only when we were told that he had died, and we came to bury him, did we find out that there had been a marriage and that, legally, he had a wife. You say she is an honest woman? I tell you she's a cunning old fox, that's what! Had she even a modicum of honesty and shame, she would not have taken advantage of his situation. But no! She approached him, perhaps even put something in his food or drink to further disorient him, and forced him to marry her, and settled herself comfortably on somebody else's property. And you still call her honest? And then it is I who is labeled dishonest, I—accused of eating people up alive! That's what you get, Natalka, for your soft heart, and for trying to live in accordance with God's laws."

There was some truth in what the woman was saying and Andriy's anger at her melted like frost in springtime. He now better understood the hatred that this aggrieved person had towards his friends and the reason for her wanton behavior towards the "family" she had never wanted. But he also knew the other side of the story, and that is why he continued to advocate on behalf of the Hrechaniuks. He told the woman how the whole situation had come about, and assured her that Mrs. Hrechaniuk was an honest woman, who did not want to hurt anyone.

"She will vacate the premises on her own," he promised, calling on God as his witness. "Only don't throw them out now. Wait until it gets warmer, and they are able to look for and find another place to live."

Natalka Kuzmenko softened somewhat, but mistrust still had a strong hold on her soul because her life experiences had not been easy.

"I'm worried that I will be duped again," she replied. "Lodgings are hard to find these days. People ask forty rubles per month for a small hut with no windows. How would she be able to afford such a price? If I let them stay on until springtime, summer will follow closely on its heels, followed by the fall, and then the winter cold once again. They'll stay here interminably! And we need that shed. After all, when you have a house and garden you must have a place to store rakes and shovels and your other junk, perhaps. Where else could we store them?"

Andriy boiled over in anger.

"You ought to be ashamed of yourself, *titka*!" he shouted unexpectedly. "You would throw out two people and condemn them to a certain death so you can have a place to store a rake and some other junk? And you say that you carry God in your soul and have a warm heart?"

"Oh stop! I'm not condemning anybody to death!"

"Yes, you are! You would want to throw them out into the street in the middle of winter!"

She continued arguing futilely with Andriy, and finally came out with her trump card.

"And what if they burn down my shed and house? I can't be here all of the time to keep watch over them. A kerosene stove is always a hazard. Who do we have there? One of them is very young, the other very old, and both are inexperienced. They've never laid eyes on a kerosene stove in the village. It's a recipe for disaster!"

"If you are worried that something bad will happen, then please give them permission to cook in the house from time to time."

"That's taking things a bit too far now," replied Kuzmenko. "Since the beginning of time no two women ever got along sharing their house and their kitchen!"

"Perhaps that is why they now have to get along stacked up by the hundreds one on top of the other in one common grave," replied Andriy gloomily. "Isn't that so, *titka*?"

"There's no guilt of mine in that!"

"We are all guilty, *titka*, all of us! We are guilty because not only do we not extend a hand to the drowning, we even give them a good push to send them further away from the shore and from safety. In the village, when the campaign against the *kurkuls* was unleashed, didn't their closest neighbors fight over their belongings like dogs fighting over a bone? They fell all over each other, over every article of clothing, every piece of furniture, and even over the potted plants. Where did it get them? They all ended up leaving behind both the goods they looted and their own possessions, and went out looking for death on the roads."

There was something so bitter and painful in Andriy's voice that Kuzmenko shuddered and became very pale. She kept looking at Andriy with eyes filled with horror and remained silent. Andriy, too, fell silent.

In another moment, he brushed away the images he saw in his mind, and spoke again, softly and passionately:

"*Titka*, believe me. *Baba* Hrechaniuk would sooner die than ask for your help. For two days now she has respected your wishes. She sits with her grandson in that shed without turning on a light or lighting the stove, eating only dry bread and water. I am a stranger to them, perhaps more of a stranger than you are, but I beg you on their behalf. Do you hear, *titka*? I beg you, as I would my own mother, have mercy on them. Don't cause them any more pain. Please! They've been badly burnt by life already."

With these words Andriy raised her stained hand to his lips. Such ardent words, and such an unusual, for these times, demonstration of respect completely disarmed her. The woman shuddered again, and, holding back tears with difficulty, said in a broken voice:

"Yes, let them be. Let them cook and sleep in the house, while it is cold outside. We will not be able to move back in here for at least another month. My husband is angry with me. We haven't spoken since the funeral. He said he would not go against the law and will not throw anybody out by force and, if I insist, he will not raise a finger to do anything in the house. So I'm painting here just to get back at him. Actually, the walls here have to be prepped, and the tile stove needs to be renovated. It is almost completely burnt out and crumbling inside."

"So you say they can cook here?" asked Andriy, interrupting her impatiently.

"Yes, let them cook and sleep inside. Then we'll see. We'll see what God wills, and that's how it will be."

Andriy quickly stepped out of the house and called out:

"Hey, Hryts!" he shouted. "Bring your pot here! Time to start cooking the barley soup!"

Hryts at first did not believe him, but when he realized that Andriy was serious, he was there in an instant. Actually, the pot made it across the threshold first. Only then did Hryts appear. Looking fearfully at Kuzmenko, he greeted her and walked over to the stove. He placed the pot on the very edge of the burner, as if it were a meek supplicant sitting on a low stool in front of a person of high position. Hryts's grandmother came in a moment later, caught him by the hair and pulled it straight up to its full length.

"God help me, ma'am!" she said to Kuzmenko. "Did you not hear what I said?" she screamed at Hryts. And again to Kuzmenko: "You see how children have become today!" And then to Hryts: "By what right are you slinking up to someone else's stove, trickster?" And to Kuzmenko: "Please don't be angry at us. He will never cross your threshold again." Then she shot back to Hryts, "Off you go home, rascal, before I show you where crabs spend their winters!"

Mrs. Hrechaniuk was alternately turning to face Hryts and then Kuzmenko, all the time pulling on Hryts's hair with one arm while trying to hold Andriy off with the other as he tried to free his friend from her grip. Poor Hryts bobbed about like a puppet on a string. Finally Kuzmenko intervened and stood between the boy and his grandmother.

"Leave him alone, sister-in-law!" she said, holding *Baba* Hrechaniuk by the hand. "I've given my permission. Cook!"

Mrs. Hrechaniuk got so mad that she took a step toward the other woman. She seemed to want to catch her by the hair as well, but restrained herself:

"Don't you call me sister-in-law, young woman!" she said, raising her head proudly. "We are not sisters-in-law, you hear?"

"Oh? But didn't you . . . ."

"As a child, I was given the name Sydorova at my baptism," interrupted *Baba* Hrechaniuk. "But for the last forty-two years I am known by my husband's name, Mykolaivna Hrechaniuk. This will be the name with which I will report to God when my time comes!"

Now it was Kuzmenko who felt insulted.

"Was it really so shameful to carry the name of Manchenko? True, my deceased brother did drink too much, but it was misfortune that drove him to it. He came from honest folk. He never harmed a soul in his life. He'd been a good person from his earliest years. He was the kind of person who would have allowed the tips of his fingers to be cut off, if in so doing, he would have helped another person."

Mrs. Hrechaniuk objected.

"The tips of his fingers? Why, he would have given his whole arm! Manchenko wasn't just a good person; he was a saint! He saved my grandson and me from certain death, risking his life in the process. I will be praying for him to the end of my days, and as earnestly as I pray for my own father."

They went on in this way, each finding yet another thing to praise in the deceased man until they finally threw themselves into each other's arms, kissing and sobbing together till the whole house shook.

Hryts was watching the women, scratching his head and winking to Andriy. Gallantly he pushed the pot to the middle of the metal plate over the stove and threw in a few branches to rekindle the dying fire.

"Now we will have enough food to make up for the three days of hunger!" he exclaimed to Andriy.

But Andriy had picked a good moment some time earlier to slip out of the house. He had to go to the market and buy a few things so that, when *Baba* Lidia returned, he would have something good for her to eat.

Baba! Andriy's heart contracted in deep, deep pain.

10

Again the days went by slowly in futile waiting. A jug of steamed milk, topped with a lightly browned layer of fragrant cream, stood on the shelf in the hall, along with a quarter of cooked chicken in a covered bowl. In Lidia Serhiyivna's room, a fragrant yellow lemon rested on her bedside table. Andriy had paid a total of 11 rubles for these purchases at the market. He spent another 3 on rolls, and an additional 3 on an old alarm clock. But Lidia Serhiyivna did not return home, and the clock turned out to be unneeded. Now that he no longer had to report for work at the factory, Andriy did not come home as tired as before. He no longer fell into the couch and into a dead sleep. These days, when he did turn in for the night, he found it difficult to fall asleep. He tossed and turned for hours, ears cocked to every sound outside. He would drop off into a semi-conscious state sometime before dawn, but then would wake up again and lie there for a long time before the alarm went off.

He would get up unwillingly, force himself to have a little something to eat, and then force himself to go to school. Only on the way home did the hope of seeing a familiar welcoming light in the cracks of the window and smoke curling up from the chimney put a spring back into his stride. As his hopes were dashed again and again, a sense of deep unhappiness settled upon him, and despair marked his soul. It became unbearable to sit at home all alone. But he did not want to go out, either. He could have dropped in on Mrs. Nestorenchuk, but the thought never even crossed his mind. He had had no desire to tell the Hrechaniuks everything. He was grateful that his *baba* had never come up in the conversation during his last visit. No, he really could not go out. In spite of everything, he lived in a state of continuous anticipation. His anticipation was always greatest at night.

Lidia Serhiyivna did, indeed, return at night. It was a night just before the weekend. The weather had once again turned frigid. The hardened earth clearly echoed the hum of an approaching car. The hum of the motor ceased for a few minutes in front of the gate.

Andriy quickly got up, and struggled to put on his shoes. He strained his ears, every muscle in his body taut, his heart in his throat and thumping loudly all the way up to his temples.

The car started up again and left, and there was a feeble, uneven knock on the gate. Andriy bolted out like a shot, quickly swung open the gate, nearly pulling it off its hinges in his haste. Lidia Serhiyivna stood there, holding on to a post. Something in her demeanor stopped Andriy from joyously greeting her and screaming out "*Baba!*" He bundled her up in his arms and quickly carried her inside. She was very still in his arms and strangely light, feeling not unlike a little rag doll. Were it not for the heavy crackling of her breathing, he would have thought she was dead.

Andriy laid her down carefully on the bed, and then went out to the close the gate, shut the door behind him, and only then turned on the light. He took a look at her and his hair stood on end in horror. Was this really *baba*?

On the pillow lay a yellow unfamiliar swollen face with watery bags under closed eyes, with blue—almost black—lips, covered in pink foam. *Baba*'s old black hat had slid to the side of her head, loosening some strands of her grey hair.

The first thing that came to Andriy's mind was to give her some water. But the semi-conscious woman could not swallow it. The water did not reach her throat, and trickled, mixed together with pink-colored saliva, down the corners of her lips.

"Help! Doctor!" thought Andriy, biting his lips so as not to scream out loud. Where to run? Whom to call? What to do? Looking at this live corpse, which was lying on the bed motionless, Andriy only now understood what it means to be really solitary.

Baba Nestorenchuk! That's whom he would call! He looked at the clock; it was getting close to 2:00 a.m. No matter. He jumped out into the street without bothering to put on a coat and ran to the house across the road. He knocked for a long time before a frightened-angry male voice answered.

"Who's there?"

"It's I, Andriy, grandson of Mrs. Cherniavska. Is *Baba* Nastya home?"

"What happened? What do you want?" the woman answered immediately.

"For the love of God, please come! *Baba* may be dying! Come to her, please, and tell me where to find a doctor!"

"She's actually back? Oh, dear God! You . . . I . . . run along home and I'll follow you in a short while."

She kept her word and came quite quickly, running straight to the ill woman's bedroom.

"Oh horrors, what have they done with you, my golden missy? You have had to endure torture, like Christ on the Cross. You are hardly recognizable. May they suffer as much as you and never find peace, those who did this to you!"

Lidia Serhiyivna's face contorted in pain and irritation. She lifted her hand a little, and let it fall down again. Noticing this, Andriy pushed Mrs. Nestorenchuk out of the room and into the kitchen.

Tortured. Tortured! The word was like a knife cutting into his brain. This was the word he had not allowed entry into his consciousness until now.

"Hush now!" he hissed angrily. "Stop whining! Tell me where to find a doctor."

"I've sent my son-in-law for one already," sobbed Mrs. Nestorenchuk.

"Which doctor? Where?"

"Dr. Nepyjvoda. He was a friend of Dr. Cherniavsky's. He's an old doctor. A good one. Not like these young ones, who know next to nothing."

"Does that doctor live far from here?"

"Yes, far. Very far. They might be able to catch a trolley here, perhaps. In the meantime, we should heat up some water."

"Should I take *baba's* shoes off?"

"Yes, and her clothes, too. She'll need to be carefully undressed and washed. The whole house stinks of prison already, if you'll pardon my saying so."

Only then did Andriy notice that the house truly reeked of something heavy and unpleasant, something that reminded him of the smell of the orphanage.

Waiting for the water to boil, both Andriy and Mrs. Nestorenchuk tiptoed to the door of the bedroom and listened carefully. Lidia Serhiyivna lay motionless, but she was breathing. She allowed herself to be undressed, and finally even swallowed a few spoonfuls of water, but turned her face away when offered milk. She would cringe impatiently and fearfully at every sound. Mrs. Nestorenchuk's constant muttering and crying as she tended her patient was disruptive to her peace. Andriy, too, found it irritating. It called to mind the wailing people did at funeral services. He was beside himself with anger and a kind of superstitious fear.

Finally, he could stand it no longer. He stopped Mrs. Nestorenchuk before she entered the room and threatened:

"*Baba* Nastya, you must stop this whispering and this crying. If you cannot be quiet, then you had better go home!"

"But I cannot stop, son! I cannot!" she whispered, managing to just put the boiling water down on the table before she dissolved into tears. "When I recall how she was as a young woman, and look at her now . . . . Dear Lord!"

But then she took hold of herself, drank a glass of cold water, and washed her tear-streaked face with a moistened corner of her apron, and said, resolutely:

"All right, now. I won't anymore," she promised. "If she is not crying, then I don't have the right to cry either. Stay here. I'll prepare the room for the doctor's visit myself."

Andriy, too, did not cry. The last two tears he shed were when he read the announcement in the papers about "the liquidation of criminal cells that had been organizing furious protests against collectivization." He had to admit, though, they had not been restorative tears, the kind of tears that made one's soul feel better. Actually, the last time he truly cried was on the road from Hrun' to Okhtyrka when he was wailing in sorrow over the death of his father. Once he was in the orphanage, however, he did not cry. Only the little ones and the sick ones cried there, those who had recently been torn away from their families. Even these children soon learned to stop, for crying did not help. It did not touch anyone. On the contrary, it invited scorn and cruel treatment. It was in an orphanage that, in the words of Shevchenko, "the tears of youth dried up." Tragically, Andriy matured way too early, and lost what was to have been the spring of his childhood years. He forgot about crying, and about laughing, too. When was the last time he had laughed?

Though his heart had hardened, it still hurt, not unlike a callous—the harder it got, the more sensitive it was to each touch. Listening attentively to each breath, each sigh coming from Lidia Serhiyivna's room, Andriy felt a ball of sorrow forming in his throat, which threatened to break loose in a scream: They tortured her to death! To death! I bet her body is crisscrossed with wounds to which her blouse had become glued.

Lidia Serhiyivna did not scream or even sigh much as Mrs. Nestorenchuk bathed her. One heard only the sound of splashing water and the gentle murmuring of Mrs. Nestorenchuk, as she bathed the woman who had been her employer not so long ago:

"Yes, my dear. Yes, my darling missy. I'll wash the other little hand now too . . . Now, I'll turn you to the side and wash your back. Don't try to move yourself, don't strain. I'll do it myself. Yes, yes, that's the way . . . . Relax . . . ."

Baba Nastya worked for a long time, speaking softly the entire time. Finally, she was done. She brought out the basin, along with a bundle of dirty undergarments, and placed them in the hallway.

"I'll take this home to wash," she explained, answering Andriy's querying look. And in a whispered aside to Andriy, "She was not beaten. There are no marks." Then she continued, more loudly:

"I saw a lemon somewhere. Perhaps we could make some tea."

Lidia Serhiyivna drank the tea with relish, and this greatly encouraged Andriy.

"A little more, *Baba*?" he asked.

She managed to shake her head no and whispered with difficulty, "Later . . ."

Dr. Nepyjvoda arrived only after four in the morning. Tall, handsome, blue-eyed, with a shock of white hair on his head, he filled the house immediately with his presence and his loud bass voice. He asked no questions. He wiped his hands carefully with alcohol, picked up his big medical bag, and went into the bedroom with the air of a man who knew his way around the house.

"Do not follow me," he ordered. "And do not listen at the door! If I need you, I'll call you."

He examined Lidia Serhiyivna for nearly an hour, and when he finally emerged, he was white as a sheet. Nervously, he rummaged in his bag, taking out little packages and jars from his medicine bag, his hands trembling all the while. Looking at him, Andriy began to shake, vainly trying to shoo away the growing feeling that his suspicion was slowly turning into certainty.

Finally, finding what he was looking for, Dr. Nepyjvoda ordered, "A spoon and water!"

"Maybe tea?" asked Andriy timidly.

"Water!" shouted the doctor impatiently, adding in a quieter tone, "We can give her tea a little later."

He stirred two spoonfuls of the powder into the water and carried it into the bedroom. Coming back, he put his hands over a washbasin, and Mrs. Nestorenchuk poured some water from the jug over them. Drying his hands, he turned to her and said:

"You, Tymofiyivna, should go home now and relax."

"Oh! You still remember me?" she responded, all aglow.

"I remember that you have very big ears!"

Mrs. Nestorenchuk immediately simmered down. "And a very short tongue!" she fired back.

"Your tongue has to be shortened as well. If you don't do this yourself, others will do it for you. Go home! God be with you!"

Left alone with Andriy, the doctor mellowed a bit. He turned to Andriy and said:

"Lidia Serhiyivna will be sleeping now. She needs nothing at the moment. Do not open the shutters, don't wake her up, don't ask any questions, don't talk, and don't let Tymofiyivna into the house. Do you understand? I will come again this evening. You should lie down also and sleep for at least two hours. You hear?"

Dr. Nepyjvoda noticed the jar of milk on the table and asked, "Have you any bread?"

Totally surprised, Andriy took out the bread. The doctor poured a cupful of milk, sliced off a piece of bread and handed it to him.

"Eat!"

Andriy was completely at a loss.

"Eat, I tell you! I haven't got time to dawdle with you!"

He was not joking. He was really angry. Andriy had to comply. He chewed the bread hastily, drank it down with some milk, while Nepyjvoda sat, tapping the table with his fingernails as if to urge him to eat faster.

"Well, now you can lie down," he said, when Andriy finished. "Conserve your energy. You will need it."

11

Andriy woke up just before noon and quietly padded barefoot to Lidia Serhiyivna's room. She was still sleeping, face turned to the wall. Her breathing was still heavy and hoarse, but not quite as labored as it had been during the night.

Without putting on his shoes, Andriy lit a fire, took out some pots and started cooking as many kinds of food as his meager supplies and poor culinary skills would allow. He moved like a shadow, and tried to do everything as quietly as possible, so as not to wake Lidia Serhiyivna. He stopped every once in a while to tiptoe to the door, and listen in to her breathing.

It was almost evening when she woke, coughing. In an instant, Andriy was beside her. He helped to turn her in the bed, fluffed up her pillows, adjusted the down comforter and, mindful of the doctor's warning, spoke as little as possible. The tone of his voice and the love with which he cared for her said more than words ever could. Lidia Serhiyivna could not but feel how much he loved her. Choosing a good moment, she took hold of his hand and held and stroked it. With this gesture she, too, said more than she could ever have said with mere words.

"So you see, I am home again," she said.

"*Baba*, don't talk. You're not supposed to. It's against doctor's orders. He will be here soon. I will bring you something to eat now."

She probably did not have much of an appetite, but she tasted everything in order not to hurt his feelings—the chicken consommé, a bite or two of the roll, two spoonfuls of porridge, and even a piece of meat. Then she drank the pear compote with evident pleasure and thanked Andriy.

"Now I will sleep," she said.

Dr. Nepyjvoda arrived at that very moment. Andriy immediately informed him that Lidia Serhiyivna was better and that she had even eaten. But somehow, Dr. Nepyjvoda did not share Andriy's happiness.

"Good, good," he murmured, without much conviction and with evident impatience. "Are you going to school tomorrow? You must go!"

"Who will stay with *baba*?"

"You will have to find some woman to be here in your absence. But not Tymofiyivna. Do you know anyone who doesn't talk so much?"

Andriy shook his head, but suddenly remembered—Mrs. Hrechaniuk!

"I do know someone like that," he said. "An honest and good woman, and she lives nearby."

"Well, run and make the arrangements with her, then, while I stay here. Ask her to come very early tomorrow morning."

"Perhaps she should come and stay overnight?"

"I said tomorrow morning!" replied the doctor brusquely. "Be on your way, but . . . hold your tongue."

Andriy had the feeling that the doctor wanted him out of the house for some reason, but he did not protest. Obediently, he dressed and left.

The Hrechaniuks were still living in the shed. (Mrs. Hrechaniuk clearly had not accepted Kuzmenko's offer to live in the house.) Hryts opened the gate for Andriy, and Mrs. Hrechaniuk came out as well. Less out of curiosity and more out of politeness, she asked if his grandmother was truly very weak and what had happened to her. Noting that Andriy answered evasively and in very general terms, she asked nothing more, promising only to come early the next morning. Hryts would bring her.

Arrangements made, Andriy returned home. The doctor sat smoking and blowing smoke into the open door of the stove. He listened only with half an ear, or perhaps not at all, to Andriy's account.

"Have you had your lunch yet today?" he asked unexpectedly. "Of course not, you've forgotten. Heat up some food, for I am hungry as well."

He threw the cigarette butt into the stove and started rummaging in his bag, taking out various little packets and bags. Among them were rice, oranges, real tea, and other things.

"This is for your *Baba*," he said sternly. "We'll eat whatever you have there."

Andriy wanted to look in on Lidia Serhiyivna, but he would not allow him to.

"Don't trouble her! She will sleep some more!"

127

He threw himself on the food like a hungry wolf, and swept everything off the plate, seemingly without even knowing he was eating. Andriy was forced to eat as well, bending to the iron will of this man, who issued commands rather than spoke, and who erupted in anger at every attempt to wiggle out from under his power. Andriy guessed that Dr. Nepyjvoda's anger was only a mask for a great fear that held him in its grip. It was fear that caused him to behave in this way. Nepyjvoda remained silent, and tried to avoid Andriy's gaze in every way possible.

"I will sleep here tonight!" he said curtly when he was done eating.

He took out another cigarette, opened the door to the stove, and lit up. Andriy washed and dried the dishes. Silence reigned in the house.

Finally, Andriy lost his patience.

"Doctor, what happened to *baba*?" he asked cautiously.

Nepyjvoda looked at him sideways and took a big puff.

"Tell me, doctor," persisted Andriy. "Did they torture her into this state or did she contract an illness on her own?"

Nepyjvoda nervously threw the cigarette butt into the stove, slammed the door shut, and jumped to his feet.

"Naturally she took ill all by herself!" he uttered with bitter irony. "Who would dare to torture with impunity an old woman in our 'most just, most happy, most humane country in the whole wide world!' Lidia Serhiyivna took ill all by herself due to her own carelessness!"

He kicked the chair angrily, shoved his hands into his pockets, and sat down. Andriy got up. He came up to Nepyjvoda with his fist clenched and fixed a look full of hatred and menace into his blue eyes.

"Doctor," he said hoarsely, "don't make fun of me! Tell me the truth!"

"Truth!" again the doctor smiled a sad bitter smile. "The truth here, you fool, would only be a mockery of the truth. So if I were to tell you that your *baba* is suffering from traumatic hepatitis, kidney inflammation, and that she is spitting up blood and has bronchial, and many other problems, would you be able to make sense of it? No, neither would I!"

"So they actually did torture her!" moaned Andriy.

"There's no proof of that! And even if there was, it would be of no help at all."

Andriy felt weak in the knees. Catching hold of the corner of the table, he sat down slowly. He felt goose pimples over his entire body and his palms were moist with cold sweat. He lowered his head and sat silent for a very long time.

"My late grandfather once told me," he said slowly, "that at one time people passed their own judgment and punishment on horse thieves and murderers. They would tie a plank of wood to the guilty person's back and beat on that plank with the butt end of an axe or a beater. There were never any marks left on the body, but the person would start vomiting blood, and would die a few weeks later."

The doctor scornfully curled his lips.

"In your grandfather's time, Andriy, people were still very ignorant. Science has made great progress since then. Today, even people who know next to nothing about physiology can stump even the most experienced doctors."

This sarcasm, which bordered on cynicism, could drive a person mad, and Andriy had a great desire to throw the doctor out of the house. But, looking more closely at Nepyjvoda's pale face, his trembling lips and shaking hands, he understood that the doctor was making a superhuman effort to keep his true emotions under control. Had he not taken refuge in cynicism or anger, he would have had to either break down in sobs or break up the house in anger. This thought immediately helped Andriy make his peace with this odd and severe man, whom he already quite liked despite his fear of him.

"Doctor," he asked, pleading. "Tell me truthfully. Will *baba* live?"

"One month!" barked Nepyjvoda. "Maximum two! But she can die at any moment."

Although Andriy was already prepared for it, this sentence, delivered in such an authoritative voice shook him up so badly that the doctor, catching a glance of his pained face, lost control of himself and exploded:

"And what did you expect, you brainless idiot? You thought I could perform a miracle? All her vital organs are mutilated, and it is only her iron will that is keeping her alive. Even the most modern medicine cannot explain such a phenomenon, and only stands by, gawking idiotically!"

Nervously he paced the kitchen back and forth, and then quietly added, "Lidia Serhiyivna knows everything. She is, after all, the wife of a doctor and has worked in a hospital herself at one time. She cannot be fooled. And she shouldn't be fooled. That's only for the weak-spirited. Her soul is forged of steel."

He sat down and spoke in an even quieter voice.

"If I am not the stupidest doctor this profession has ever known, then I foresee that your *baba* should feel better for a couple of days, barring . . . barring any new and sudden surprises. Even if she does feel better, don't delude yourself with any false hopes. You will save yourself another great shock. Now that you have become this woman's grandson, follow her example. She told me about you. Not this time, but back then, when she was running around trying to arrange the whole business of your documents."

Then he looked at Andriy, who was silent and despairing, and again became angry.

"Why are you just sitting there, like a doe!" he slammed his palm on the table. "Dumbfounded, are you? You've never looked death straight in the face before? May the devil take the entire clan of you Pivpolas, proud descendents of a line of Cossacks. Scream, threaten, promise to avenge, cry, whatever, but don't just sit there, still as a rock!"

Andriy raised his head and looked at Nepyjvoda severely.

"The Pivpoly are not people who scream and flail their hands about," he said quietly. "Pivpoly cry only in childhood. Cherniavska's grandson must follow her example.

Nepyjvoda lost control. He rested his bushy-haired gray head in his hands and wept.

12

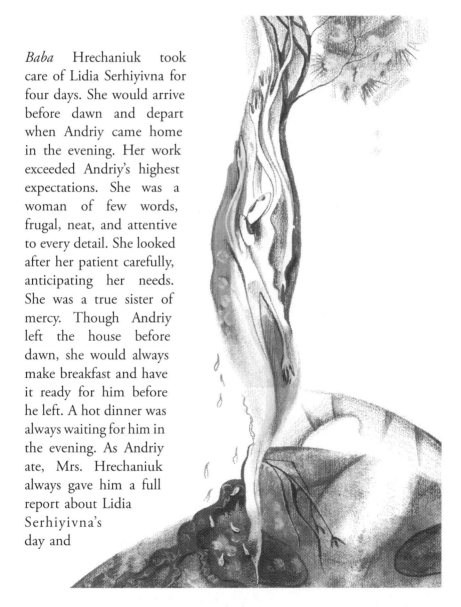

Baba Hrechaniuk took care of Lidia Serhiyivna for four days. She would arrive before dawn and depart when Andriy came home in the evening. Her work exceeded Andriy's highest expectations. She was a woman of few words, frugal, neat, and attentive to every detail. She looked after her patient carefully, anticipating her needs. She was a true sister of mercy. Though Andriy left the house before dawn, she would always make breakfast and have it ready for him before he left. A hot dinner was always waiting for him in the evening. As Andriy ate, Mrs. Hrechaniuk always gave him a full report about Lidia Serhiyivna's day and went over her plans for the following day. Only then would she leave for the night.

The first thing Andriy did when he awoke in the mornings was to run to Lidia Serhiyivna's room, always fearing the worst. Some days, he found her still sleeping, on others, she'd be up and asking for the time. She said she was feeling better. It was clear that she was telling the truth, for her voice had become stronger and clearer with each passing day. Still, both of them knew this recovery would not last very long; neither of them said a word about it.

Dr. Nepyjvoda came every evening. He would go straight to Lidia Serhiyivna's bedside, spend half an hour with her, and always emerge with a worried expression on his face. He prepared her medicines and administered them himself. Then he would sit near the stove in the kitchen and smoke. He rarely spoke with Andriy. On the rare occasions they did talk, it was always about trivial things. Dr. Nepyjvoda always sent Andriy off to bed a little after 10:00 o'clock, while he himself kept vigil through the night. Most often, he sat in the kitchen, dozing off from time to time. Sometimes he would spread his coat on the floor and stretch out on it. Andriy offered him the couch, but that just made him angry. Dr. Nepyjvoda had a key to the house, and he usually left before Mrs. Hrechaniuk came, or shortly thereafter.

That weekend, Andriy had a "*subotnik*" at school—a Saturday when students were required to report to school to do some "volunteer" work. The day was to be spent cleaning the school classrooms. However, only half the students, and none of the master craftsmen, actually complied with the order and showed up, much to the displeasure of the janitor and watchman. The students who did show up spent their time tidying up the workshops, and putting things away in a rather haphazard fashion. After sweeping up the floors, they decided their job was done, and left.

The sun was shining hotter than it had the weekend before. Large chunks of snow and sheets of ice slid off the rooftops and into the streets. Rivulets of water flowed on both sides of the streets. Even this inhospitable, smoky and dusty city started to give off the sweet-smelling fragrance of the approaching spring.

The usual happiness that accompanies the awakening of spring was missing in the city this year. The shabby black silhouettes littering its sidewalks, looking ever so much like a large number of pieces of charred paper that had been swept in by the wind, draped the city in the rather dreary colors of mourning. These huddled-together-groups were more numerous on the sunnier side of streets. They had converged there in greater numbers, searching out the warm rays of sun to warm their freezing and hunger-emaciated bodies. They were still searching, still feeling, and still eager to hold on to life, even as it was draining out of them.

Andriy came home after ten o'clock in the morning. He was surprised to see that the shutters in Lidia Serhiyivna's room were open and that a generous shaft of sunlight streamed in through the window. He noticed, too, a distinct smell of decay that lodged itself in his throat.

"What's this?" asked Andriy in fright. "What happened?"

"Nothing happened. I merely opened the shutters," replied Mrs. Hrechaniuk calmly. "She asked me to open them. Said she found lying in the dark tiresome. She wanted to see the sun."

While Andriy was washing the black mineral oil and rust off his hands, Mrs. Hrechaniuk gave him an update. Lidia Serhiyivna had asked her to wash her and to comb her hair. She had eaten little and had taken her medicine.

"Maybe I should go to the market now?" she asked when she finished. "I need to buy a few things for you, as well as for my own home."

"By all means, go!" Lidia Serhiyivna chimed in unexpectedly from the other room. "Do what you need to do at home and come back in the evening. Andriy will stay with me now."

Andriy escorted Mrs. Hrechaniuk to the door, and hurried back to Lidia Serhiyivna. Since her return, he had never seen her by the light of day. He took a good look at her now, and again became uneasy. Her face was no longer swollen, but it was more wrinkled than before and her skin sagged. She had aged, and her skin had taken on a strange dark hue. The stamp of approaching death was clearly on it, leaving little room for hope. The heavy smell of death was more powerful than before.

"Sit down, Andriy," she said, smiling weakly. "I want to talk with you."

"Dr. Nepyjvoda forbade you to speak, *Baba*," said Andriy, struggling with all his might to control his emotions.

"Oh, it doesn't matter anymore," she said with a dismissive wave of her hand, adding, "You know everything, don't you?"

He knew. He saw it on that darkened face. Still, he made an attempt to pretend that he did not understand.

"I heard," he said, turning his head away, "but I do not believe Mrs. Nestorenchuk."

"Mrs. Nestorenchuk?" Lidia Serhiyivna looked like she was struggling to remember something. "Oh, you mean Nastya! She's one of those people who gets sick if she is unable to find out what one neighbor or another is making for dinner. She's a good soul, but much too inquisitive."

"Well, she did not get any information out of me," said Andriy. "She, however, talked up a storm here!"

"I remember she was here the night I got back. Who called her?"

"I did."

And Andriy told her about his acquaintance with Mrs. Nestorenchuk.

"She said that they had taken you away because you supposedly had some kind of gold and foreign currency."

Lidia Serhiyivna raised her hand.

"Not 'supposedly,' Andriy, not 'supposedly.' She spoke the truth. I do have gold and jewelry, which I have buried. My son did send me money from Paris through *Torgsin* a while back."

Andriy looked at her in astonishment.

"Why are you so surprised?" she asked. "Perhaps you think I am hallucinating? No, no, son. I am completely lucid."

She was agitated. Her breath had become more labored.

"The secret police know about the money my son sent me. They know that I refused to accept it, and that I had sent it back a number of times. They also know that I asked him to stop sending money. The secret police read all the incoming and outgoing mail in the country. And, if the secret police know, then so must Nastya then, naturally! No, no, don't think badly of her. She has her own independent sources of information and hates the secret police no less than I do.

"As for the gold I have buried, well they only have their suspicions. They've detained me twice and interrogated me about it. Each time, they kept me a couple of days, and then let me go. Clearly, they still had their suspicions. This time, however, I have truly 'convinced' them."

She laughed a hysterical kind of laugh, which quickly turned into a bout of coughing. Shuddering, she stretched out one hand towards a bottle on the bedside table, and with the other, drew a blood-stained towel from under her pillow and pressed it to her lips.

Andriy hardly knew what he was doing, his hands shook and the medicine he was pouring onto a spoon spilled over. Still, he helped Lidia Serhiyivna sit up, and waiting for an opportune moment, gave her the medicine. She swallowed it with difficulty, fell back onto the pillow, and again pressed the towel to her lips. Then she turned sideways with a jerk in an effort to stop coughing. Her whole body shook as she coughed and rasped; she continued to wipe her lips on the towel. Andriy now knew where the stench of death was coming from. It was the smell *Baba* Nestorenchuk had dubbed a "prison smell" the night *baba* had come back. Now he understood, and he stood motionless, feeling helpless and very, very sad. He was prepared for the worst already, for he knew *baba* was condemned to die, but his whole being protested and silently screamed out in excruciating pain. He did not know what to think or what to do. Covered in a cold sweat, he stood by helplessly and mutely looking at this woman—the closest and dearest person in the world to him—whom Death had already branded as its own. He had lost his family, his childhood home, and the best years of his life. Why did he now have to lose the person who saved him from death, and who gave him shelter? Why did he have to lose her restrained, but deep and very warm heart?

At last Lidia Serhiyivna stopped coughing. She continued to lie on her side with her back to Andriy, breathing with difficulty. In time, her breath became easier. She calmed down completely and asked for some cold water and a moist towel. He helped turn her around, wiped her sweaty forehead, and handed her some water. She drank a little, lay back on the bed, closed her eyes, and fell silent. Had she fallen asleep, or was she simply resting?

Andriy carefully pulled up a chair to the bed and sat down. He was now able to think and reason more calmly. So, *baba* really did have gold she had hidden. It was totally understandable that she did not want to give it up to the secret police. In her place, he would not want to give it to them either. Many farmers had hidden grain from the government thieves in an effort to save themselves and their families from starving to death. Very rarely did the government bureaucrats manage, by threats, torture, and terror, to wrest the secret hiding place out of these people. Even when a farmer became convinced that he would never be able to use the grain he had hidden because of the large number of *seksoty* (paid informers) at every step, he still chose to be exiled, to flee the village, or even to die in his own home, rather than to hand the grain over to the government.

There were cases when government officials did succeed in finding some hidden grain. Then they would raise a cry in the media that "this loathsome saboteur, and enemy of collective construction" from such and such a village had "criminally decided to allow grain to rot rather than handing it over to the government." But the farmers saw things differently. Andriy's own father had always regretted having handed over all his grain—to the very last kernel!—to the government. "If I had known," he would say, "that we would have to die anyway, I would have hidden that grain in a hole in the ground somewhere, or scattered it in a river instead. If I can't have it, neither can they!"

Grain was bread. But gold? Why did Lidia Serhiyivna have to hide her gold when she could have taken it to *Torgsin* and exchange it for food, and not just give it away for nothing!

Andriy had finally seen one of those *Torgsin* stores with his own eyes. He had stood in front of the window salivating at all the delicacies on display. Many of the foods in the window he had never seen before, much less tasted. *Baba* probably wouldn't have even had enough gold to barter for those fancy foods, but she surely would have had enough to trade for a bag of good flour, some lard and some sugar. Probably, there would have been enough to feed herself and perhaps another starving person or two. Instead, she had allowed herself to be tortured to death. (God, what *did* they do to her there!). And now she's even happy that she "convinced" them!

Had Andriy only known where that accursed gold had been hidden, he would have dug it up with his own hands and taken it to the secret police. He would have said, "Here! Choke on it! Just don't torture *baba*. Let her go." But he couldn't do that now. It was too late. *Baba* was dying.

And then there was the money her son had sent. This was a complete mystery to him. Could they have tortured her just because he had sent money to her? After all, she didn't even accept it! Having created a *Torgsin*, where they accepted only foreign currency as payment for the goods in the store, why would they torture people for actually having foreign currency?

Lidia Serhiyivna opened her eyes.

"Now, Andriy, I'll tell you the rest," she said hoarsely.

"Don't talk, *Baba*, don't talk. It's not good for you! You'll start coughing again."

"No, I won't anymore," she replied, pointing to the medicine bottle. "Now I won't cough for at least two hours. I have to . . . I want to . . . talk. Soon I will be silent for all eternity. If I only had a little more strength, I'd go outside to say my goodbyes to this world. The day is so beautiful, so sunny."

She noticed Andriy's face, all contorted in pain, and lightly touched his hand.

"Do not be sad, son. I will be better off in that world than you will be in this one. I will pray God to give you a better fate, a better fate for you and for everyone."

He carefully took her cold w i t h e r e d palm and rested i t against his face. He wanted to cry. He wanted so much to cry that he was almost screaming inside. He wanted to cry hard, to sob and let all the pain out. But he did not dare. He had no right to impose his pain on this dying woman. Lidia Serhiyivna understood him. She lightly caressed his face and with the greatest calm reminded him that no one lives forever, and that only people who do not believe in God are afraid to die, and that dying is nothing more than a transition to immortality.

Listening to her words, Andriy calmed down, though he could not shake off his feelings of sorrow.

"I know all that," he said. "But it would be better if you could live longer, or at least if you died your own, natural, death."

Lidia Serhiyivna smiled wanly and asked mockingly, "And whose death am I dying? Someone else's?"

"Stop joking around, *Baba!*" pleaded Andriy, getting a bit angry. "I was thinking that if I had known about that hidden gold of yours, I would have taken it to those thrice-cursed murderers myself in order to set you free!"

Lidia Serhiyivna brusquely pulled her hand out of his.

"It's a good thing that I did not betray my secret to you earlier," she said angrily. "For you would have committed a sin for which I would not have forgiven you even in the afterlife!"

"No, I wouldn't have! God commanded us to help our neighbor."

"So you would have wanted to light one candle to God, and another to the devil?"

"Why to the devil?"

"Because! Do you know why the Bolsheviks are trying to track down all gold and foreign currency? You don't? Let me explain. It's because their state is as impoverished as 'the starving.' True, the Kremlin leaders and their henchmen all over the country are sated and live in luxury, but they know that the people hate them, and that they are perched on top of a volcano. To hold on to their power, they have to feed an army of secret police, informers, and *parttysiachnyky*.[28] This costs money. Of course they have to have an army to back them up. But an army without arms is no army at all. So they have to have weapons: rifles, shotguns, machine guns, cannons, tanks and ammunition. To transport all of these from place to place they need trucks, trains and planes. To manufacture arms and build

---

[28]   See footnote 26 for an explanation of *parttysiachnyky.*

transportation networks, they have to develop heavy industry, so they need machines. To purchase machines, they need money. Soviet rubles have no value on the world market because they are not secured by anything.

"You might find this difficult to understand, for you haven't studied economics yet. Let me explain. For currency to have value, it has to be secured either by manufacturing goods, by agricultural goods, by natural resources, or by gold. The USSR has only natural resources."

Andriy listened attentively and silently, though he thought to himself that, even though he hadn't studied economics, he'd gotten some insight through his work at the factory. The "heavy industry" at that factory was indeed in poor shape. The country's agricultural sector—well, it was on the streets and roads, begging for bread. Things had gotten so bad the year before that someone had made up a ditty people were singing: "No cows, no pigs, just Stalin in picture stills." This year, there was no one left to sing at all. Many had died, and others were waiting their turn tomorrow or the next day, or the week after. The economy was going nowhere.

Lidia Serhiyivna went on, as if giving a lecture.

"Even after they achieve their goal in this country, the Bolsheviks will not feel safe as long as they are surrounded by another world, what they call the 'capitalist' world. So they have decided to conquer the world. For that they, again, need money. You cannot foment revolution abroad with worthless Soviet paper. Propaganda campaigns, the organization of strikes and revolutions, provocations against governments and their leaders—all require a solid financial base. That's why they are hunting for gold, why they've opened up *Torgsins*. That's also why the cities have also been placed on hunger rations. This is all designed to force people to give up all their valuables, all their reserves. The secret police order people who have families abroad to write and to ask for as many dollars or other hard currency as possible. They say this openly: 'Our government needs money!'"

"Well, now I understand why you sent back the money your son sent!" said Andriy.

"You do? Well, thank God for that! I don't have to explain it any further to you. The secret police, however, did not understand. And thank God for that as well!"

"They did not understand?"

"No. I told them that I was afraid to accept money from abroad, lest it bring me trouble." And she explained: "Say I receive money from my son. They accuse me of getting money from a capitalist group abroad in exchange for information and spying."

"Hmm . . . yes, that does have a ring of truth to it, I must admit," said Andriy.

"Yes. They tried to assure me that this would never happen, that they would even give me a guarantee in writing."

"A guarantee!" Andriy smiled scornfully. "Who would place any trust in their guarantees!"

"That's precisely what I asked them: whether they had even managed to get any guarantees for themselves and their own lives. I reminded them that the leaders who had given my husband a guarantee have been executed a long time ago."

"You said that to them, *Baba*?" asked Andriy, elated.

"Yes, I did."

"And they? What did they say?"

"Nothing. They were insulted, of course." And she closed her eyes.

"Insulted?" exclaimed Andriy. "That must have cost you dearly."

Silently he sat looking at that old tired face and was ready to kneel before her and pray, as one would in front of an icon. What a person! What a woman! So feeble, so small, yet so strong in spirit, like the Cossacks of old he had read about. Dr. Nepyjvoda was right when he said that her soul was forged from steel. She was a good person. His own mother could not have been better to him. And now she lay dying.

"*Baba*," he said reproachfully and with great pain, "you did not place a high enough value on yourself. You saved me because I was reciting a couple of lines from 'The Kobzar.' But you know so much more, and you are so much more courageous than I am. Why did you let them destroy you? You are not able to bring down Communism by refusing to give them your gold. Thousands, even hundreds of thousands, have handed over their valuables to them. So your gold could not have made much of a difference!"

Lidia Serhiyivna raised herself up from the pillow at these words.

"People give them their valuables because they think just the way that you are thinking right now. Or they don't think at all!" she said in an almost hostile voice, and lay back down again. "How many years has life been teaching us, and to no avail? Oh yes, I know. More than one mother has bartered her wedding band for food at *Torgsin* in order to be able to feed her children a little bit better. She doesn't realize that the government will use that wedding band to fashion shackles for her children, that every gold cross will become a new Golgotha for her son, that every gem will help them to build a new prison, every pin will buy a new tool of torture, and the golden coins they spend will support secret police operatives and *seksoty*, the very people who will keep their children, at least those that survive the famine, that is, in chains.

"These mothers don't think about this. And, if they do, they pacify their consciences by saying, 'Oh, everybody is doing it. A little more, a little less will neither help nor hurt Communism.'"

"Ah, *Baba*, but what if a child is dying of hunger and there's no other way?"

"And those who don't have anything to barter or sell, what are they to do?" she fired back, looking at him sharply.

She was right. What could they do? Andriy could not find an answer, and remained silent.

Lidia Serhiyivna paused for a while, and then said:

"Ever since our ancestors lost their fight for independence, we have rarely fought. More often than not, we are on the defensive and try to protect ourselves. Now, we are no longer even protecting ourselves; we are just dying. Standing on the edge of annihilation, we are nonetheless giving weapons to our mortal enemies, which they will be able to use against us, against our children, and against the whole nation. Some give them gold, others—their consciences, all just to prolong their miserable lives. I am surprised that my Borys, an intelligent and educated person, does not understand such a simple matter, and attempts to sweeten my life at the cost of harming other lives, including his own children's."

"It's because your son knows that you are worth a thousand people! Perhaps that is why he wants to save you!" exclaimed Andriy passionately.

Lidia Serhiyivna's lips parted in a barely perceptible smile.

"If indeed I am worth something, Andriy, it is precisely because I am guided by certain principles. Do you not understand that? Look. Suppose I took the money my son sent. Suppose you and I shared some very good meals and lived very well, though, as I have already told you, you would have to pay a price for that. And then suppose that fate, on one and the same chain, bound you and a person who had never had the opportunity to even take a whiff of a product you bought at the foreign currency store and consumed. Suppose that this friend in misfortune says to you, 'You helped forge this chain by taking such good care of your stomach. Why must I, too, be bound by it, when I had no part in the pleasure?' How would you answer him?"

Again Andriy did not have an answer.

"You remain silent?" asked Lidia Serhiyivna. "I'm not done yet. Those parcels from abroad would separate us from others, adding another layer to the walls that already exist between people because their ration cards give them the privilege to buy different amounts of bread. People whose ration cards allow them 150 grams a day are jealous of those who get 250 grams, those who get the lesser amounts are jealous of those who get 400 grams, and all of them are jealous of those who get 600 grams. And the starving are jealous of anyone who can have 100 grams a day to eat!

"Imagine how much jealousy surrounds the people who get parcels from abroad? Ever since the rumor that I get money from my son spread, my neighbors use their eyes to drill holes into every basket and every packet I bring home. The mailman pretends that he does not recognize me, because he expected that I would reward his bringing 'happy news' from abroad by giving him a gift of a cup of semolina or a cup of rice for his child. He did deliver several communiqués from *Torgsin* to my address, after all, and he has no way of knowing that I sent the money back."

She asked for some more water, closed her eyes, and lay motionless for a while. Andriy, keeping track of her every breath, also remained silent. But his thoughts were racing, getting all tangled up in a knot that was not easy to undo.

"*Baba*, are you asleep?" he whispered.

She shook her head. "Do you want to say something?" she asked.

"You are always talking about gold and foreign currency. But what about those who work? Take, for example, me. Didn't I work at the factory fixing steam engines for the benefit of the enemy?"

Lidia Serhiyivna opened her eyes.

"I've told you already, Andriy, that the devil takes his tribute from each of our actions. But we cannot allow ourselves to be turned into illiterate manual laborers, as our enemy wants. By working, you are learning, and we all need to learn. Schooling, even if it is at the hands of the enemy, can always be turned against him. So continue learning. Learn and spite the devil!"

She suddenly became very animated.

"You know, Andriy, your questions remind me of a fantasy of mine, a dream, which has not given me peace for a long time."

"A dream?"

"It is clearly unrealistic and silly. But if approached with total faith, we could still win, even at this late stage."

She met Andriy's enthusiastic and at once questioning gaze and smiled somewhat guiltily. Then she took a deep breath.

"Imagine, son, what would happen, if one fine day all forty million Ukrainians, together with the smallest children, declared a hunger strike."

"A hunger strike?" repeated Andriy, wide-eyed. "But we have hunger already!"

She shook her head.

"This is something different, son! I am not thinking of a forced famine that has been deliberately foisted on the rural population of this country by the government. I am thinking about a voluntary hunger strike by the whole nation. This would mean that all the people in the country would stand shoulder-to-shoulder in solidarity with 'the starving.' They would throw away all their ration cards, boycott all the stores, and not come out to work!"

Andriy became excited, and wiped his forehead.

"Well," he said, hesitating, "the government would probably be only too happy if everybody threw out their ration cards. But, not work? They'd call out the army and shoot everybody!"

"You are wrong, Andriy. The government would be more afraid of a hunger strike than of any other strike. Naturally, they would unleash a campaign of terror. However, they would not be able to execute more people than the number currently dying of hunger. Stalin can destroy seven or even ten million people. But forty million? No! Can you imagine what that would mean? How big an army would you need, how many bullets, how many graves, grave diggers, cemeteries? And we—we are not alone. There are other nations: the Belarus, the nations in the Caucasus, the Asiatic peoples. The army, too, is not exclusively Russian."

Andriy's excitement increased with every word. With every word, the idea seemed more realistic and easier to execute. Lord, this is so simple! Not to go undercover in partisan movements, not to form secret organizations, like those Committees of Self Defense, but to proclaim openly: "We are prepared to die. We do not want your government or your laws!" Why hadn't people thought of this before?

"*Baba*," said Andriy, bending over Lidia Serhiyivna and taking her by the hand. "This truly would be a way to save ourselves. What's needed is for everybody to stand together!"

Lidia Serhiyivna sighed sadly, very sadly.

"For people to stand together, Andriy, requires preparation, and preparation requires an organization that is even larger, even stronger than the Committees of Self Defense."

"What for?"

"What for? And how were you thinking of going about it? How would you communicate with 40 million people even about setting the date and time for the hunger strike?"

She was right. How? Andriy brushed his hand roughly over his forehead, thinking hard. He could not find an answer. Lidia Serhiyivna, in the meantime, continued speaking.

"Never before has any nation been in the situation we are in right now. And there's no way to fight back. We have no weapons, and our soldiers are forced to do their military service in areas beyond our borders: in Russia, Siberia, Asia, in the Far East . . . What can we do? We can only call a general strike and a hunger strike. This, too, requires time and organization. And the time is very unfavorable. Who will you rouse to fight—the millions of half-dead people? No, no, this is not something that can happen now. This is for a matter to be taken up in the future. That is why I told you the first time we met: suffer, endure, and wait. But wait intelligently, and don't stop dreaming. All great deeds start with a dream."

Andriy's excitement died down, like a torch that had been plunged into water, and changed into the bitter smoke of disappointment.

Lidia Serhiyivna suddenly became troubled.

"Oh my goodness, Andriy. We've brewed up a storm with our talking, and I haven't yet told you, and you haven't asked, where my valuables are hidden."

Andriy could not contain his frustration.

"I am not interested!" he said, shrugging his shoulders.

"Your indifference is commendable. Had you been different, I would not have spoken of it. Now listen. My gold is buried under that pear tree outside. It is down very deep. There was once a well there. There's a nine meter drop to the water, and the water goes down another meter and a half."

Though uninterested and otherwise dispirited, the idea of the secret hiding place excited Andriy.

"Is that the same well you hired people to fill up?" he asked.

"Yes. I see Nastya has told you about that as well."

"Yes, she did."

"Does she know that I put my valuables in there?"

"No, she doesn't. She said that they took everything away from you when they robbed you during the revolution."

"Oh, so she knows about that too?"

"Well, that's what she told me."

"What a woman!" said Lidia Serhiyivna, shaking her head. "She was living here while I was living on Sumska Street at that time! But, God be with her! They did rob me of everything, but this robbery was never called by its proper name. It was called 'requisitioning.' Luckily, the 'requisitioners' were people who could not tell the difference between real gems and ordinary glass, so they took the copper for gold."

For the first time in many days Andriy burst into hearty laughter.

"So you gave them . . . ?" he left the sentence unfinished, slapping his knee with his fist.

"Yes, and I even made them give me vouchers for everything they took!" said Lidia Serhiyivna, smiling. "When the revolution broke out, our friend, a jeweler, advised us to take the precaution of making imitations of our valuable jewelry. We followed his advice and bought half a bag of such imitations, and this is what later saved me. Still, I had a great deal of trouble over it. I had to hide with these goods, stay away from home for weeks at a time, until everything quieted down."

"After that they resettled you here?"

"Yes. That's when I threw my valuables into the well."

"And you filled up the well later?"

"Not until some three years later. And only then did I regain my peace of mind. I put my valuables 'under lock and key' and 'closed myself away from them,' much like you once wanted to hide yourself away from 'the starving' who kept knocking on the door. Now, even if I wanted to, I could not get to them. The well simply cannot be dug up in secret. There are too many snooping eyes around."

The long conversation had tired her. Her voice became weaker and weaker. Her purplish-black eyelids closed over her eyes more and more frequently. Her breathing became more labored.

"Andriy," she uttered with effort. "All my valuables are in three earthenware jugs that have been wrapped in tar-covered fabric."

"*Baba*," he said sorrowfully and took her by the hand. "Don't talk to me about the gold. I've no interest in it."

"You are a silly boy!—'I've no interest!' If you had my valuables during normal times, you would be a rich person. There are enough gems and gold in there to exceed one hundred and fifty thousand Tsarist rubles. You could buy the whole factory you worked in with that amount of money!"

Andriy hadn't expected that, and his eyes widened.

"That much?" he asked, though without much enthusiasm. But in his mind he had already figured out that this amount could purchase thirty thousand bags of the finest rye flour!

"It's quite a bit. I had tried to let my children know in my letters to them about how much these valuables are worth and where they are hidden, but they did not understand my hints. Obviously, I couldn't just tell them outright. So, I'm 'giving you the key' to the treasure."

"To me?" asked Andriy, frightened. "And what am I to do with it?"

"That will be up to your intelligence and your conscience. I always believe that the times will change, and my children and grandchildren will return."

"You have grandchildren?"

"Yes, four of them. Borys has two girls, and Virochka—a son. And then there's you."

"Me?"

"Of course. You want to disown me when I'm dying?"

"*Baba*," he knelt down and rested his head on her shoulders, "I do not want your gold, I don't need your gems. I need you to live!"

She sighed and began to stroke his head.

"That is not up to me, son, and you must come to terms with this. My last wish is for all of my descendants to divide my valuables equally among themselves—children, grandchildren, and great-grandchildren. And do not forget: you are also my grandchild! Now, please give me some of that medicine."

She took a double dose of medicine and lay down again.

"Yes, my grandson," she reiterated. "It's you I think about most often. The other three live in a free country, and have parents to take care of them. But you have no one and live under the hammer and sickle. When I die, they could take the house away from you because you are a minor. Or they could bring another family to live here. Before that happens, let's take in Mrs. Hrechaniuk and her grandson. I have come to like her, and Hryts can be a friend to you. Tomorrow we'll start working on getting them registered here."

Her words were like symbolic nails being hammered into her coffin, and Andriy had to clench his teeth hard so as not to cry out.

"One more thing, Andriy," she added in a completely exhausted voice. "When I die, write to *diad'ko* Borys. Dr. Nepyjvoda knows the address."

"*Baba!*"

"All right now, son, tell me later. Now I must rest . . ."

Epilogue

The last petals had fallen from the pear tree, covering the earth in a thick carpet of pink and white. It seemed like nothing more was left on the tree but, with another gust of wind, another cloud of tiny pink and white helpless butterflies fluttered to the ground. They lay at the foot of the tree, sadly moving their delicate and partially-torn wings every time a warm current breathed a little bit of life into them.

On the streets of cities and in the fields, ravines and villages in the rural parts of the country, the petals of the life of millions of Ukrainian farmers were falling. Not white and pink against the earth, but black, like the soil these farmers had worked generation upon generation, like the black soil which had nourished, not only them but the country as a whole, and people in distant lands as well. They fell, and fell, and fell . . . . Lord, God, where will it end? When will You still the skeletal hand of the implacable reaper gathering this bountiful harvest even now, after the frost and cold of winter have passed?

Winter was coming to an end. The sun was shining brightly in the heavens, and the earth hastened to meet it with the smiles of greens and flowers, while the famine raked in ever higher and higher mounds of corpses. Blossoming May, the month that from time immemorial celebrates life, was now a holiday in which death prevailed.

Diagonal rays of evening sunlight are streaming down, searching out the grasshoppers in-between the green crowns of sprouting potato plants, among the rows of cabbage, and the beds of curly lettuce. Birds chirp, a radio blares in the distance, and steam engines angrily roar at one another at railroad stations. Andriy is sitting on a bench working, half-listening to Hryts's chatter in the garden. He's averting his head in disgust from the smell of frying fish that is wafting in through the window from the kitchen. He cannot stand the smell of this type of fish, the cheapest fish on the market. It calls to mind the acrid smell of corpses. He knows that

Baba Hrechaniuk will be bitterly disappointed that he won't be having dinner once again.

At that very moment, Borys Cherniavsky, an engineer, is sitting in a charming villa in a Paris suburb, chain smoking. He, too, is irritated, but by the smell of mushrooms in sour cream, asparagus, and a pork roast. He, too, knows that he will not be eating dinner this day. He has not been able to work or eat for two days now because of the letter—that unexpected, sad, and at once senseless and impudent letter.

So, mother has really died without seeing her children again, and without getting to know her grandchildren, whom she had met only on photographs. This was painful enough. But the rest of the letter! It was signed "the son of your sister, Tetiana." What an arrogant, cynical lie! Borys knew that his sister Tania (diminutive of Tetiana) had never married and had no children at the time of her death. He had learned this quite by accident when he ran into an old school friend, who had run into Tania when both of them were fleeing the Revolution by way of Siberia, Manchuria and China. This friend told Borys that he had buried Tania with his own hands. She had died of yellow fever. Borys had never written his mother about this, not wanting to pain and grieve her unnecessarily. And now this "nephew" shows up!

Upon recovering from his initial shock, Cherniavsky read and reread the letter with rising indignation. He knew from the press what was happening in Ukraine, and he came to the conclusion that his mother had taken pity on some young man, had taken him in, and had taken him into her confidence, speaking about family matters with him. And now this rascal wanted to capitalize on the information. In his next letter, this young man would probably ask "*diad'ko*" for money, which he will accept, unlike Borys' proud mother, who always sent the money back for reasons that were a complete mystery to him.

That mother had ever even thought that this lad could be the son of her daughter, Tetiana, was completely preposterous. Had she believed such nonsense, she would surely have written to share this happy news with the rest of the family. Of course, the correspondence between them had ground almost to a halt these last several months. Mother had discreetly let them know that keeping up any international ties could be a problem at the moment. Still, in a case like this, she would surely have let them know. No, mother was too intelligent to be taken in by some barefoot lad. More than likely, she later sorely regretted having given shelter to such an impudent person. It wasn't unlikely that he had taken advantage of the elderly lady's illness to force his way into the house. The letter said she had "been gravely ill for five weeks." She might have taken him in because she needed help, someone to look after her. And he . . . what a scoundrel! A scoundrel! It was not difficult to imagine how she must have felt dying in such company. Might he even have had a hand in hastening her death?

Still, how strange that letter was. Written in a neat, half—childish hand, with no spelling errors, it had the deranged quality of an emotionally ill person. "*Baba's*" death was described in only a few sentences, without crocodile tears, without false sentiments or expressions of pain (thank goodness that this charlatan did not have enough gall for that!). And more than half of the short letter was devoted to tales about water pipes, and a well that had been covered over, pears . . . . Was this because he did not have much to say, perhaps, or was it because he wasn't altogether balanced?

There was the sound of hurried steps on the path, and a fifteen-year-old girl came in, with the now-familiar piece of paper in her hand.

"*Tatu* (father)," she began excitedly.

"Lidusiu (diminutive of Lida), please do not disturb me!" he replied irritably.

"I have no desire to speak about that scoundrel now."

"But, *tatu*, this is very important!" she insisted.

"Enough!" he shouted, his anger rising. "Let's burn this horrible letter and forget about him!"

But Lida was unshakeable in her resolve.

"*Tatu*, can't you listen to me calmly, please? I wouldn't disturb you if this wasn't important!"

She was obviously excited, and spoke so seriously and decisively that it was impossible to refuse her.

"What is it, child?" asked her father, giving in, but obviously annoyed.

Lida sat down next to her father, the piece of paper in her trembling hand.

"Some time ago, you told us how you once searched for treasure under an old tree on your property near the Lopan' River. Wasn't that a pear tree?"

"Oh, Lida, I don't remem . . . Well, actually, I do . . . . Yes, it was a pear tree. What about it?"

"And didn't you say that *babusia* had some valuables of rare beauty?"

Cherniavsky's eyes suddenly lit up with comprehension, and he snapped the letter from his daughter's hand. He scanned it quickly and paused at the sentences that had seemed totally absurd.

Earlier, *baba* had difficulty drawing water up from the well. The well was about 9 meters deep, perhaps more. But later, the Soviet government made some progress, and brought in water lines. Now we take water from the tap on the street. *Baba* covered over the well with soil, and planted a pear tree in the center. She said that you used to love the old pear tree overlooking the Lopan' River. Only that was a tree in the wild and did not bear fruit. This pear tree, however, is grafted, and *baba* has fertilized the ground around it well. It has always been her hope that you would come one day with your whole family and eat as much as you want of it. Now that *baba* is gone, I will take care of the tree to make sure that it won't dry up, so that it will be here when you come.

Cherniavsky read and reread the letter. Then, he read it again, and then yet another time. His hands trembled and his eyes filled with tears.

"My smart and wise daughter!" he exclaimed, embracing and kissing Lida. "My dear Sherlock Holmes!"

"So you understand, *tatu!*" she said with a trace of pride in her voice.

"Understand? You should better ask how I failed to understand from the very beginning. It's so very clear! Wait, Lidusiu! Yes!" He wiped his forehead. "*Babusia* was always trying to tell us something in her letters, but in spite of all her hints, we could never make out her meaning. If it were not for this boy, the secret would have died with her. He told us her secret, even though he could have kept it to himself. Oh Lida, I am so ashamed!"

"Yes, we were very unfair," agreed Lida. "For some reason, those pears reminded me of the treasure immediately."

"Treasures, jewelry—they are not so important, Lidusiu!" interjected her father. "What's most important is that your grandmother died in the arms of an honest and intelligent person. I'm still sad, but half the load has lifted from my heart."

He jumped up and, shaking the letter in his hand, shouted out through the open window:

"*Sianyu* (diminutive of Oksana), we really do have a nephew! More than a nephew—a son! Lesia, you and Lida have a wonderful brother, simply wonderful!"

Translator's Note

I have been privileged to have someone like Lidia Serhiyivna in my life. Her name is Oksana Miakowska Radysh, and she is the curator—and indeed the soul—of The Ukrainian Academy of Arts and Sciences in America, which her father founded back in 1945 in a Displaced Persons (DP) Camp in Germany, and which, since 1950, made its home on the west side of Manhattan. Oksana has worked at the Academy tirelessly and with great dedication for many decades.

Oksana was 12 years old and living with her family in Kyiv at the time of the famine, and she well remembers that time. She remembers the incessant and insistent knocking of the starving at the door. (She still marvels that, weak with hunger, they climbed three long flights of stairs to reach her family's apartment in search for food.) She remembers the straitened circumstances in which most city dwellers lived during the famine, and how there simply was not enough food (or living space or water) to go around. She remembers "feasting," like Andriy with the Savchenkos in this story, on "odbyvni" (called "dolki" in Kyiv)—the dumplings made from potato peels (for there were no whole potatoes to be had) and "baked" directly on the stove top (for there was no butter or oil for frying). She remembers the trucks that carted away the scores of corpses that were gathered each day from the streets of Kyiv. She remembers how her parents forbade her to play outside—there were hunger-crazed people on the streets. She remembers all too well the feeling of helplessness bordering on madness . . . .

Oksana also remembers the good times before the famine, when the people of Kyiv loved to go to the villages on weekends to listen to the Ukrainian songs that filled the air and enjoy the festive Ukrainian hand-embroidered clothing that the people in the villages liked to wear.

And she remembers how the villages fell silent, drained of life.

Like Lidia Serhiyivna, Oksana has a wonderful spirit. She, too, has a treasure she has kept safe—the Academy's rare manuscripts and books—(forbidden reading in post 1928 Soviet Ukraine) which her father had salvaged and preserved for future generations from the books refugees carried with them as they fled their country during World War II.

Many scholars and students have come to conduct research at The Academy, and to drink deeply of the well of knowledge and warm hospitality that Oksana keeps there. Hers is a spirit and great grace that prevails in all times. This is the spirit that Olha Mak describes so well in this book.

ACKNOWLEDGMENTS

My thanks to Ihor Mirchuk for his concise and most informative Foreword, and for some fine final edits; to Leo Iwaskiw for an initial reading of the manuscript, and for pointing me to the translations of Shevchenko's poetry. I am indebted to Franek Rozwadowski for his reading of the manuscript with a critical eye and a keen ear for language at the early stages of the work, and to Myroslawa Hec for her invaluable input. Many thanks to Olha Kowal for carefully proof reading the text. Thanks to Assya Humesky and Anna Procyk for help in identifying some key fragments of Shevchenko's verse. Last but not least, a great many thanks to Larissa Kyj, who commissioned this work and supported it throughout.

Vera L. Kaczmarskyj
Reykjavik, Iceland
February 2011

ABOUT THE TRANSLATOR

With a keen interest in Ukraine and East Central Europe, Vera Kaczmarskyj, has worked as an editor, a journalist, and a translator specializing on Ukraine and on themes related to Ukraine. This is her first translation of a book written for a younger audience.

ABOUT THE AUTHOR

Olha Mak (1913-1998)

Born and raised in Ukraine, Olha Mak and her family fled to freedom during World War II, resettling in Curitiba, Brazil, in 1947.

For a writer like Mak, who worked in Ukrainian on Ukrainian themes, making a living as a writer in a foreign linguistic milieu was not easy. Nonetheless, with grit and an unfailing belief in her vocation, she remained true to her calling. In the 23 years she lived in Brazil, she wrote for various émigré publications throughout the world, and authored several books, many short stories and numerous articles.

It was only in 1970, however, when Mak moved to Canada, that she felt, as she wrote, "my ship has finally made its way to a quiet harbor . . . ."[29]

Canada's generous social programs gave her a sense of financial security and a feeling of safety for the first time in her life, granting her peace of mind as she continued to devote herself to her craft. The active Ukrainian cultural life in Canada was fertile ground for her muse.

Stones Under the Scythe drew on Mak's first-hand experience when, as a 16 year old teacher in a remote village in Ukraine in 1929 and later as a university student in Kharkiv in 1932-33, she witnessed the step-by-step destruction of the *selo* (village) by the Bolsheviks, and the unimaginable atrocity that followed, the *"Holodomor."* It was then that she came to understand the years of careful planning that had gone into the Soviet intent to break the backbone of the Ukrainian nation with a single blow.

The images of the brutality and terror of collectivization, the destruction of the *"selo"* and the famine that followed, indelibly carved themselves on Olha Mak's soul. She was able to write about these events only many years later when she was living in the West.

The book she wrote was first published in Ukrainian in Canada in 1973 as *Kaminnia pid kosoyu* . It was immediately hailed as the best book for young adults on the *Holodomor*. Mak hoped that this story, presented largely through the eyes of Andriy and his benefactress, Lidia Serhiyivna, would reach young readers in a way that lessons in workbooks and articles or lectures on the topic might not.

Publication in Ukraine had to wait until 1994, three years after the proclamation of Ukraine's independence. It then went through several printings as Ukrainians went about the difficult task of debunking the lies and falsifications that had been common currency under Soviet rule.

This is the first English-language translation of her work.

---

[29] From Halyna Kyrpa's Foreword to the 2004 edition of this book that was published in Ukraine.